REBEL BLOOD

T.J WALKER

Proisle Publishing
1177 Avenue of the Americas, 5th Floor, New York, NY 10036, USA
info@proislepublishing.com

ISBN: 978-1-7375255-9-2 (sc)

TABLE OF CONTENTS

DEDICATION

This book is dedicated to my partner in life Yvonne. She knew I could write, so she got me off my backside and encouraged me to do it.

I would like to say sorry for all the temper tantrums I had while writing the book. Yvonne calmed me down and encouraged me to continue, saying "Don't start something you will never finish." As my Grade 7 school teacher once predicted: "One day you will do it."

Thanks Yvonne and 'Teach'. Love you both.

FORWARD

Governments do many things they hope voters will never find out about. At times some of these things (deals that are cut) have a bigger impact on the people than they realise.

Rebel Blood outlines a combination of these deals that have gone wrong.

This story is fictional but, as the old saying goes, 'Truth is stranger than fiction'. People, no matter who they are or what road they walk in life, are mindful that it's not only Governments who are wheeling and dealing. Every business does the same. It is the separation of bad deals from good deals that people want to become a reality.

About the Author

I served in the military for many years. After taking my discharge I became a Public Servant.

When I first joined the army I was not very well educated and lacked a lot of social skills. The people I call mates from the army educated me and developed my social skills. For that I will always be indebted to them.

Through my life I have tried to learn from everyone I came into contact with. I believe every person has something of value to offer (After the army I would like to say especially the lawn bowlers I ran into when playing the game!)

If life is a learning curve, then people I know have been the best teachers. It may be simple things, but all worthwhile in the jungle of knowledge. I love my Country and never want it to be destroyed. I will fight to my last breath for Australia and its people, no matter what.

  If I see something wrong I will speak out.

CJ, my editor. What can I say about a person that can transform my rough notes into a readable item? I love working with you and find that we click in a certain way; it is like you know what I am trying to say and fix it up. Love you CJ

  Love to all my Fellow Australians.

All characters, events and locations in this book are fictitious. Resemblance to anyone alive or dead is purely coincidental.

Review from Kindle Publishing

I have now had the opportunity of reading and evaluating the material relating to Rebel Blood which was a very impressive piece of work; impressive from a professional perspective and enjoyable from a personal one. It is as good a political adventure book as I have had the pleasure of reading in some considerable time.

Basically, your book has all of the qualities necessary for success in this genre. Crucially, the plot is excellent with enough twists, turns and red herrings to keep the reader interested and involved right up to the denouement which is unexpected yet wholly believable. The characters, too, are credible 'real' people who interact and behave in a way that makes reader identification very easy. Jillian is a particularly powerful yet gentle protagonist with whom it is very easy to empathise and I can envisage the reader identifying with her very strongly indeed. It is somewhat unusual to have a female as a central character in a book likes this but, because you succeed in his element admirably, it is something that will elevate the book over and above other in the same genre.

One of the book's great strengths is its pace and this is largely due to the nature of your writing, Your style is perfect for the genre and the narrative rattles along at breakneck pace, never giving the reader the opportunity to rake breath, ot, more importantly, get bored.

Also critical to the plot is the dialogue and here, once again, your books does not disappoint at all. Your dialogue is highly realistic and absorbing everything that takes place. In this respect the book is a very 'visual' one and would, therefore, be relatively easy to adapt as a film. It is well known that film makers now spend time looking for books that would adapt readily to the big screen and yours would seem to tick most of the boxes.

Your book has severtal advantages in terms publications; it is highly professional, in a very popular niche genre, expertly written and with it a significant 'following; for you personally. Interestingly, it also has tremendous televisual and, as I said, it is now well known that not only the major publishers but also television and film makers trawl the books looking for suitable material.

CHAPTER ONE

A bitter wind in the nation's capital suddenly added ferocity to the early morning temperature of minus 3 degrees. The lawns around the lodge, crisp and white, cracked underfoot as Marcus began his gardening rounds, tending to frost bitten roses and other plants that detested the cold.

He knew he would lose many plants this year and his budget, already half spent, would be strained even further to replace them.

The Lodge was home to the Prime Minister and a showpiece to the rest of the world. Marcus liked the PM. She was sexy; the second ever female to make it in the male-dominated political world. He had served two previous leaders, including her father. Then, six months ago, Jillian grabbed power. Won the election. Unlike the other Prime Ministers, she was not a 'yes' person, and often defied party aspirations; she listened to the people.

A white Commonwealth car with C1 plates slowed as it reached the pick-up point in front of the Lodge, from which Jillian emerged, wrapped in a large woollen coat. She made her way to the rear door of the white Ford LTD, already opened by her driver. After a muted greeting, he gently closed it and two Federal Police cars appeared from the side, taking up their positions, one in the lead, one behind. As the small motorcade moved off, Jillian went over the daily agenda papers her PA had handed her, and was startled to see the Indigo Project among them. If there was a leak from Indigo, she knew she and her party would never govern again.

Over twenty years ago, her father had struck the Indigo Deal with the United States of America in exchange for party funding. That was the extent of her knowledge. Jillian was not sure she wanted to know more, but she was aware that their funds kept her and the party in power.

'Do you prefer the rear or front entry?' the driver asked, as they swung into the final two hundred metres of driveway leading to Parliament House.

Jillian's eyes flashed to the front steps. There appeared to be no media snipers out gunning for 'yes-no' replies to questions she was sometimes at a loss to answer. At her political induction, an instructor drummed into her 'At all costs, avoid yes or no answers. Skirt around 'leading' questions; stick with the prepared party response. Never waver or you will crash and burn.' Jillian knew this meeting was point blank confrontation - a round table meeting with gloves off. She cast her eyes over the briefing papers again, gaining speed on the topic poised to dominate the day's discussions, scanning the list of outsiders who were poised to strike in the inner sanctum.

Jillian's anxieties gained momentum as she remembered what young John her son had asked her again yesterday. He wanted to meet his father. She was not sure if John was alive or dead.

Her own father, when still Prime Minister, had told her one night that her son's father had been reported MIA on Devils Rock. That was twenty years ago. She had believed him. Young John was raised by her parents. Jillian's father didn't want his daughter to have an out of wedlock child. He believed this would jeopardise his quest for his daughter to be the nation's second female PM. Only a few close family friends knew about it. Jillian wanted to keep it that way, but feared her son may rebel in his search for his father.

Receiving no answer to his question, the driver chose the front entry to the House of Parliament.

An ABC reporter approached, and fired his question. 'We've seen photos of the dog tags of twelve men supposedly missing in action on Devil's Rock in 1995. When is the parliament going to expose their fate, and can you confirm that your boyfriend was the commander of that unit?'

Jillian quoted the party line. 'It has not yet been confirmed if the tags belonged to members of that team of brave men. I have never dated a soldier so the answer to your question is a clear no.' Brushing past, she relaxed a little as she reached the security of the inside of the building.

Her Federal Police body guards ushered her past the other reporters gathered like a sharks' feeding frenzy. This was the part of public life Jillian detested. Making up lies on the run, then trying to cover her arse when some unrelenting reporter tried hi-jacking her answer later on.

Sometimes six months elapsed before she was confronted with the question she originally dodged.

Walking toward her office, Jillian wondered how the hell the reporter would know who she dated twenty years ago. More to the point, how much more did he know? She spun around, thinking she'd ask one of her bodyguards to get the reporter's name, but decided against it.

Jillian walked through a pristine outer room into her own inner office, whose decor was both modern and functional. She sat down behind her desk, her heart still pounding from the reporter's question, and glanced at the large framed photo of her father looking down on her. 'Oh Dad - what have you got us into?'

Again she flicked through the Indigo File, looking for the water-tight funding deal that had been struck for as long as Indigo was allowed to operate on Australian soil. The party was granted funding for campaign purposes. But the question was why Indigo? That patch was nothing more than desert, ridged with limestone. She knew the area from some of John's tales of the top secret training ground used for Special Ops.

Jillian pulled a photo from her desk drawer. A handsome 25 year old army Major in full dress uniform looked back at her. Except for young John, the photo was the only thing she had to remind her of the man she once dearly loved. Still loved. Even when told John was MIA, Jillian never dated again. She slipped the photo back into the drawer. A tear formed and rolled down her cheek.

Gathering the agenda file she stood up, white dress hugging her curvy body. As she walked through the outer office, Karen, her secretary, stood up, grabbed a tissue and rushed over.

'Your make-up is smeared. Hang on – I'll touch it up for you.'

Karen smiled warmly as she dabbed at Jillian's face, gently repairing the problem. 'Are you okay Prime Minister?'

Jillian nodded. 'Just one of those 'Minties moments' we women have' she laughed. 'Can't have you going to the meeting looking like the wreck of the Hebrides, can we?' joked Karen reassuringly.

'Thanks Karen. You're a darling.'

CHAPTER TWO

The PM's Private Meeting Room. Parliament House, Canberra ACT

Jillian took her seat at the head of the long table in the centre of the room, glancing at the name-tags at each place. She took the few minutes before the start of the meeting to once again flick over the Indigo file.

Dale Myers from ASIO walked in. 'Morning PM', he said, placing his papers on the table in front of his name tag. The PM looked up.

'Oh, ASIO Director! Must be expecting an interesting meeting?'

'Just here purely as an advisor to you this time Jillian. I think you can knock this problem on the head once and for all. I will run it past you once you have heard the guts of the meeting.'

'It sounds intriguing Dale.'

She stopped talking as others began to drift into the room and take their place around the table. Large photos of former party members hung on the walls, a small down-light shining over their faces. Jillian often thought that these dignitaries' photos were placed there as a pointed reminder of party allegiance; to warn against individual decisions being made in the room.

Sometimes she wished she could turn the photos over.

Jillian was stunned when her father walked into the room. He took the seat at the other end of the table that was reserved for the appointed director of the meeting. It was the chair of power; with jurisdiction to override the PM's chair at these meetings. She looked at her father and smiled at him, acknowledging his presence. He nodded back and took his seat.

Secretary of the meeting, Phil Harper, tapped the gavel. He cleared his throat. 'Meeting is in order. Director Gillman has called the meeting in regard to Indigo. It appears many of our opposition have been receiving unfavourable reports from property owners around the lease site, protesting that is blocking movement of cattle and other commodities on their way to market.'

Some of the other members looked blankly around the table, wondering what the hell a few upset pastoral lease-holders had to do with Indigo. Besides, the area was not in any of the electoral boundaries of the current government. The seat was held by an Independent and they, the current party, did not need his vote.

David Gillman took the floor. 'We nip this in the bud as quickly as we can. Mark my words, if we don't, you'll all be on the unemployment queue come next election and our beloved party will never see the light of day again. I say we tell the elected Independent we will put a road in so the property lease holders don't have to travel around the site. It's quick and simple and rids us of the problem.'

Jillian sat back, tapping her pencil on her teeth. Her father was up to his old tricks. There was something deeper. Was this another secret that only a select few would ever know about? Why a road around the area to fix the problem? What problem?

'What's at this Indigo site that has all of you in a fluster?' The PM aimed her question directly at her father. She was losing patience with him thinking he ran the entire show because of his standing within the party. He stood up and looked straight at her.

'You ungrateful little bitch! If not for Indigo, you would not be sitting in that chair now. Indigo is the Master Plan to ensure this political party holds power, so that we can build a strong nation without having the Opposition questioning our every move.'

Jillian fired back 'So, is this another dirty little secret deal that threatens to send us all to gaol? Why not bring all this out in the open and let these people know what kind of man you really are?'

'You don't understand child' he said quietly. Two followers sitting beside him chortled. 'Don't you 'child' me!' she replied hotly. Then stood and walked out. Dale followed. He could see she was in need of comfort. No one in that room was going to offer it.

'Jillian wait!' He yelled, not failing to appreciate the attractive contours of the slim figure retreating to her office.

She turned. 'Go on! Have your two bobs' worth.'

'No, I'm taking you for a coffee. That meeting was a debacle. It was uncalled for.' He could see the tears appearing in the corners of her eyes.

'Jesus! I hate my father at times. His so-called secrets drive me insane. When things go wrong, he expects someone else to fix the problem. He's not going to get away with it this time. I'll fix it, but not the way he thinks.'

'Come on, this is not the place to talk like that.'

'Put the coffee on hold Dale. Come out to the Lodge tonight. At least we can talk in private without Big Ears having his spies on me.'

'Okay. See you at eight?'

Dale managed to get a smile out of Jillian. He had been like a secret father to her son, and was one of the select few who knew the truth about John Kelly junior.

'Eight it is. Bring a good wine with you. Maybe two.'

Dale returned to the meeting, where no-one had wondered at his sudden departure. Most knew how close a friend he was to Jillian.

'She cracked the shits and ran away to hide. Typical of her,' her father David commented wryly as Dale resumed his seat.

Dale wondered how a father could be so cruel to his own daughter. David's nature was never to be kind to anyone. Politics had made him hard, and an expert liar.

Dale figured David even believed his own lies. He remembered the man before politics, when he was farming. He was just as bad then. He thrived for power. Dale had seen what David had put his family through. As a neighbour, he had seen David mould his daughter into what he wanted her to be. She would cry on the school bus some mornings, and he tried to comfort her. Still, one thing he knew about Jillian, family was family. Now the penny dropped. Her silence had been to protect his lies. Dale now wondered if she would cross the line to protect her country.

David now sat back in his chair, looking smug. Though aware of his daughter's sentimental nature, he figured she would never bring pain to the family. Exposing the truth was not an option. Dale, on the other hand, would have to be taken care of. He knew too much. David wondered exactly how much. This meeting might just reveal the extent of his knowledge about Indigo and the aftermath of Devil's Rock. Then again, he figured it was Dale who called the guards off when the change of government came about, so that no records of the 11 MIA's on the rock were available. He had also made sure all of the files and records had been destroyed. No records, no link. David smiled to himself.

'So far, no loose ends.'

David had no knowledge of Dale's own records of the entire event. He had trained the man too well.

'My best suggestion to you all' said Dale, 'is - call Indigo off. That is, if you want your secrets kept. Including Devils Rock.'
He walked from the room.

CHAPTER THREE

Phone still pinned to Dale's ear, he sat at his desk and waited for the voice on the other end. 'JK! What do you want?' a gravelly voice demanded on the other end.

'Listen, I've got the means to get your identities back, but you've got to come to Canberra.' 'Get fucked Dale. Not dealing with any pollies. How are the rest of my boys doing?'

'All good John, except Bardi. He's been in hospital, but word has it he'll be okay.' 'Been eating shit again has he?'

'No. Broke his leg. Don't you want to at least know the plan?'

'Maybe, but you are not going to tell me over the wire. So you'd better make the arrangements.'

'Same as normal.' Dale hung up.

Sandra, his wife was standing in the kitchen. 'Dinner will be ready in half an hour.'

She smiled at her loyal husband of fifteen years.

'I've got to meet with the PM at eight; sorry. Forgot to tell you when I got home. I'll get something on the way over.'

'Another good meal down the sink. We never get time to sit down and eat together. I wish to hell you'd never become director of that piss fart organisation. You're never home. The kids wonder who the hell their father is, and I wonder who the bloody stranger is in bed with me when you're home.' She burst into tears.

Dale went over and hugged her. At first she pulled away, but then accepted his arms around her.

'I'm sorry Dale. I know you serve your country to the best of your ability, and you did explain things would get like this' she said, through sobs.

'We have holidays coming up soon' he said, pleasingly. 'We'll go down to the farm; see Mum and Dad. The kids can go yabbying and we'll relax.'

'No work? Ha! Stupid question.' He laughed a little.

'Tonight I'll ask Jillian to come with us. I think you and her are going to get quite a surprise.' 'Okay. I'm sorry Dale.' She kissed him long and hard on the lips.

'I do love you.'

'Love you too Babe.' He responded to her kiss. 'Got an hour before I have to go, and

...hmmm! The kids are out.'

Sandra gently unbuttoned his shirt. She placed her hands on his broad shoulders and pushed him down onto the kitchen chair, tugging at his zipper. Sliding her knickers down, she straddled her husband, allowing his stiff penis to enter her. Dale deftly opened her blouse, exposing her breasts. He sucked on the erect nipples and flicked his tongue over them. Sandra responded as she twisted on his penis, shooting volts of arousal into his every nerve. He lifted his hips, slowly entering her fully. Sandra moaned with excitement as he expertly located her G spot.

'You know me so well. You clever dick. Oh....my. God!'

Sandra shivered; her body shook as he thrust into her, exploding with pleasure as they both came. They remained on the seat for half an hour, just holding each other.

Dale showered and dressed. He shaved and selected a nice wine from his collection. He kissed Sandra.

She whispered 'Be home early and you might get an instant replay.'

'Fast forward to that I say' he rejoiced, tapping her backside and walking to the door and opening it. His daughter and son were standing there.

'Hi Dad! Bye Dad!' was all he heard.

That was a defining moment. He realised what John junior was missing; what Jillian was missing, along with the strike team members. Family life. It was time to repair the damage he had played a part in creating

CHAPTER FOUR

Jillian was sitting in her den sipping wine when the housekeeper came in. 'Ma'am, there is a Mister Dale Myers to see you. He says he has an appointment.'

'Oh yes. Show him in please Debbie.'

Jillian always called her staff by their given names, as a gesture of respect. After all, they gave her respect. It wasn't too much to ask in return.

Jillian made sure she was respectable, fastening the top button of her blouse and putting her shoes back on. Standing up in the polished furnished room, she brushed down the front of her skirt and blouse, and then sat down again on the leather lounge.

This was Dale's first visit to the head house of the nation. He took in the things around him. The still-ferocious stuffed lion glowering at him in the passage. The elephants half leg and foot pad, now an umbrella stand. A plaque: 'From the people of Ruanda'. Along the passage, portraits of past occupants looked down like watch dogs.

Debbie stopped at the door to the den, indicating the well-lit room where the Prime Minister would receive him. He handed Debbie the bottles of wine, and stepped inside. Jillian stood up and walked over to great him.

'Dale!' she kissed his cheek.

Dale returned the gesture, wishing it was her very inviting lips that he had often longed to kiss. In high school, not long before she had met John Kelly, he thought he had won her heart. But it was never to be. Dale could smell the sweet perfume she had on. He moved back to ensure Jillian could not feel his passion building.

'How is Sandra?' she asked, showing Dale to his seat.

'Great. So are the kids. She says to say hello.' Mentioning his family checked his passion.

Appearing with a bottle of wine and two chilled glasses, the housekeeper put her tray down, saying 'If there's nothing else you need Jillian, I'll call it a day now.'

'Okay Debbie. Give my love to your family. See you in the morning.'

Gathering her coat and hand bag, Debbie began to sing as she walked to the door and out to the staff parking area to the side of the building. As she made it to her car she heard a noise. She spun around only to be grabbed by the throat. A rough voice asked her who the male visitor was. Debbie thought it was one of the Protective Service Officers having a bit of fun. Her brief stated she was never to disclose the names of the PM's visitors, so she shook her head, realising her assailant was a stranger. She tried to scream, to attract the attention of one of the officers patrolling the grounds, but all sound was stifled as her attacker's grip tightened.

Debbie kicked out, managing to connect solidly with his shin, and momentarily loosening his grip. She turned and bought her knee up into his groin. The man cursed in pain, protecting himself with both hands. He had not reckoned on the fact that this 'domestic' had diplomas in self-defence. Debbie brought both cupped hands down on the back of the man's neck, kicking out again. Bullseye! His hands hardly lessened the impact of her well-aimed strike. He backed away, hurling his choicest expletives as he felt his balls breaking in half.

Debbie ran back towards the Lodge and hit the alarm bell that would immediately summon the Protective Officers. Two quickly appeared from the side.

'The staff car park! Someone tried to strangle me!' she shouted.

Both guards drew their weapons and ran toward the staff parking area. In the distance they could make out the shape of a man trying to run, though all he could manage was a hobble.

Alerted by the guards, an anxious Jillian and Dale appeared, only seconds before the Duty Officer for the Protective Services, who sprinted to where Debbie now stood.

'What happened?' he asked.

Debbie looked at the PM then back at the Duty Officer.

'I was jumped, walking to my car. The guy asked who the Prime Minister's male visitor was.'

She then explained how she dispatched her attacker. The Duty Officer flashed his torch over Dale's face.

'Sorry sir. Didn't realise it was the Director of ASIO' he grunted with a rueful smile, deflecting the bright light from Dale's face.

A gunshot rang out. Then silence. The two patrol officers returned, dragging a man between them. They dumped the body at the Duty Officers feet.

'Sorry boss. He's history.'

The duty officer flicked on his light and shone it down at the corpse. The bullet had struck his face, which was half torn away.

'Anyone know this fella?'

Dale looked. He knew but shook his head. He'd had a run-in with this man before. It was not the housemaid he was after.

Still stunned, Jillian turned away, hiding her face in Dale's shoulder.

'Take him to the guard house and we'll start hunting down his identity.' The Duty Officer turned back to the PM and her guest.

'Sorry about all this. I'll have two men posted at the door till we find out who this bloke is and what he wanted. Debbie, you get cab charge. I'll be in touch.'

After thanking Debbie, with high praise for her courage and quick thinking, Dale and Jillian returned to the Lodge.

'Bloody hell! On the grounds of the Lodge, one of the best patrolled grounds in the Capital!' Jillian sputtered, as Dale closed the door behind them. She rounded on him.

'I could tell by your look you knew that man.'

'Not much escapes you. Yes, I busted his sad arse a few years back. ASIO knows him well.

Revenge job most likely. Come on, let's finish our wine and we can talk.'

Dale led her back to the den and sat down. He reached for his wine, drained the glass and poured another.

Jillian sat and sipped thoughtfully, then put her glass down and looked into Dale's bright blue eyes.

'So - what was it you want to talk about?'

Dale sat back. He fiddled with the cuff of his jacket. 'How much do you know about Indigo?'

'Only what the files say. Why?'

Dale figured Jillian didn't know that Indigo was responsible for her son's father being reported Missing in Action at Devils Rock. She had no idea what transpired afterward, or that John Kelly was very much alive, as was his entire strike team.

'What have you told John junior about his father?' Jillian looked strangely at Dale.

'The truth. That his father was a highly trained officer who ran a select group of men, who were all killed on operational duties on Devil's Rock. What has this got to do with Indigo? Or today's interloper?'

Dale grimaced, and then sighed.

'I bet it was your old man who told you John was killed. Did he also tell you that before the unit left for Devils, he'd asked for your hand in marriage?'

'Yes to the first. No to the last. Dale – what's going on?'

Standing, Dale walked to the sideboard and picked up the photo of John Junior. He looked down at the image of a very young boy, not older than five. It was taken one Christmas at his place. Dale's own son stood beside the timid little boy, who had been lied to all his life. Gently returning the photo.

Dale took his jacket off, hung it over the back of a chair, and sat down.

'Indigo is an American secret research base. In return for it being on Australian soil, the US bankrolls your Party's election campaigns, ensuring your Party get in over and over. You fall, Indigo falls, and the US are exposed. People discover exactly what's going on. Jillian, you are currently nothing more than a puppet government to the US. They call the shots, not you.' Stunned, Jillian slowly shook her head.

'Let me guess...dear old daddy?'

'Bingo. A year after your father lost office, the government of the day was called to account and sacked. Your old man's party was returned to power, and has remained in the chair from then to now. Indigo made damn sure of that' Dale replied, sipping his wine.

'If what you are saying is true, then...why?'

'That, Madam Prime Minister, is the million dollar question. One we need to answer if we are not going to remain a puppet to the US.'

Jillian knew he was on the level. He never addressed her as Madam Prime Minister unless he wanted her full attention.

'I figure you have a plan forming in that spy mind of yours.'

'In mind yes, but not yet fully formed. Can you join us on our family holiday in a few weeks, down on the farm? I can then reveal all. I want to make some more enquiries in Canberra before that happens.'

'I'm intrigued. I'm also shit scared after what happened tonight. But I'll see what I can dig up from my chair. I hope to God you've got it wrong Dale. This is my family and Party we're talking about.'

'I know, but it also concerns the future of the country. You as PM will have to make a judgment-call in the not so distant future; the hardest call of your life. Country or family.' Dale stood.

'Gotta go. I want to start digging from my end.'

Jillian walked him to the door. She reached up and kissed him, this time on the lips. 'Maybe it's premature, but thanks for all you've done for me and my son.'

He hugged her, and then pulled back, holding her at arm's length.

'Just stay strong and focused for me, and for him. All will be revealed soon Jillian. It's time you were free of your father's dominating grip. You'll be your own person.'

'its mum I worry about.'

'Yep. You'll need to call on that inner strength. Good night mate.'

Dale winked, walked to his car and drove off. A million things were running around in his mind. If he could pull this off, he would make his best female friend the happiest lady in the land. He was stopped at the guard house.

'Duty officer would like to talk to you sir' the gate keeper said, pointing toward the guard house.

Dale entered the guard room. The building was well overdue for a makeover. 'Mr Myers - my office please.'

The Duty Officer pointed for Dale to take a seat, and then asked for two coffees to be bought in.

'We have the low down on the dead fella. He's a Kiwi. A hit-man hired by a group in America to take you out. Wanna tell me why?'

'Sorry, ASIO Staff Commander,' Dale retorted, with playful sarcasm. Playing politics, he smiled at the duty officer.

'Well, for your sake, I hope to hell you watch your back. Last thing I want to see is your ugly dead mug plastered all over the Canberra Times.'

'Do us a favour commander?' 'Depends.'

'Work with me, not against me, on this one. See what you can get on a group called NWC. They're a rich-list mob backed by the American government. I want to know more about them and what they're up to.'

'Done. Reckon our 'stiff' was mixed up with them?'

'Maybe. Things point in that direction. Obviously, it was me he wanted tonight, not the housekeeper.'

Dale chuckled, then stood and waited for the commander to finish scribbling his notes. He extended his hand, which was accepted.

'This is between you and me. ASIO stuff, you know.'

Dale handed him a business card.

'Call me if you get something. Any time. You ever considered ASIO as a career?' 'Nah. Reckon I'm not chopped up for it?'

'May be Commander. This is your trial run. We'll discuss it again after you get the info for me. No need to dig too deep. Just find out what NWC stands for.'

Dale knew the commander had made a play for ASIO. He now had secrecy on his side. 'Maybe we'll pick up a spook along the way' he thought. 'They never go astray.'

'Be on to it first thing sir,' the commander said, with a very wide grin on his face. Get this right and he wouldn't have to apply for ASIO though the normal recruiting channels.

He placed the business card in his shirt pocket under his jacket. 'Take care, Director,' he said, as Dale walked back to his car.

This commander was a powerful man; a type he had needed for a long time. Someone deep inside the Federal Police. He hoped he could be trusted.

Dale started the engine, his mind now on the erotic 'chaser' awaiting him at home. It was only twenty two hundred hours. Early, he figured.

CHAPTER FIVE

John Kelly appeared from his humpy. His long, greying beard, which stopped just short of his belly button, fluttered in the warm breeze. In a small bag he carried what clothing he had left. He checked his pocket to make sure he had the address he would need in Darwin.

His deep-set eyes glanced over the rough terrain; at the community ute waiting to take him to the bush airstrip, then on to Darwin. It didn't feel right to be leaving. These black people had saved him from death. Fed him. Asked no questions. Fifteen years had passed since he and his team had walked out of the military police's most secret and protected prisons. They had woken one morning to find the camp guards no longer there. They simply took one of the vehicles that had been left behind and drove out.

It was not until John found a newspaper that he realised he had a hope of getting back what they had taken away. He would go public about the true events on Devils Rock. Eighteen months later, the new government had been sacked and his old nemesis was back in power. The soldiers' chances of being free again were dashed. John no longer trusted Canberra. He was even not sure of Dale's motives; even though he had made sure the banished troop stayed hidden from the grip of politicians who were determined that John Kelly and his team would remain in exile. However, Dale sounded sure he could pull it off this time. With hesitation, John stepped onto the back of the ute.

'When you're ready Billy!' he shouted to the driver. The vehicle lurched forward and began its bumpy journey toward the dirt airstrip.

The flight to Darwin took an hour. John looked down on the country he once would have laid down his life for. Now he was a total stranger in his own birth land. The light aircraft touched down gently on the long black airstrip at Darwin Domestic, and taxied to its parking point. 'Your taxi is organised. He'll meet you at the arrivals lounge. The driver will be holding a card with JK on it.'

The pilot remained behind, shutting down the twin engine Cessna.

John walked the short distance to the lounge. He stopped at the drinking fountain and took a sip of water. He noticed the curious stares of his fellow travellers. Not surprising that a half dressed white man would attract attention. He returned their incredulous stare, sniffing his underarm as if to say 'The smell is not from me.'

'Why don't you take a photo? It will last longer.'

Many of the people instantly looked down, realizing that the roughly dressed 'hobo' was affronted by their ill-concealed curiosity.

'Don't worry people. I'm not going to jump you.'

The crowd dispersed, leaving John standing alone. Glancing around, he saw a 'JK' sign, held by a young, well-dressed Aboriginal taxi driver.

'JK, that's me.' He introduced himself to the driver.

'Well JK, the taxi is this way,' he grinned, showing his row of white teeth that looked like he had just come out of a dentist chair. 'My name's Jimbo.' He smiled again, taking John's small bag from him.

'Jimbo, you wouldn't have a fag would ya?'

The taxi driver gave him a packet. 'Boss told me to bring some.' 'You must be one of Dale's new boys.'

'Yep. Dale figured no white taxi driver would let you in his vehicle, so here I am.' Jimbo drove expertly through the traffic, pulling to a stop at a men's tailor shop.

'You've got new clothes waiting for you.'

'Thinks of everything.' John got out and walked into the shop. Once again he could feel people's stares. He looked around as they tried to pretend they were not looking. John swung around and glared defiantly. The shop soon emptied. Laughter erupted from behind the counter. 'Well fuck me! John Kelly, the wild bushman! The one they couldn't root, shoot or electrocute. I've got your bundle here, and your play money.'

John took the bundle of clothes then shook hands with Ralph. 'Thanks for that last delivery of whiskey you organised.'

'Not a problem John. You're booked into the Darwin Hilton. I've got a shower out back if ya want to clean up before you wipe yourself out at the bar over there.'

John thanked him and took the offer. He was soon standing in clean matching clothes that perfectly fitted his every sinewy contour. The shoes were a battle. His feet were long unused to being encased in leather. Looking in the mirror, he was tempted to shave, but put the razor back in the small toilet bag. He picked up his bush clothes and walked back out to the shop front. 'Size bigger in the shoe I think. Got a bag for these?' he asked placing the old clothes on the counter.

Having replaced his shoes for a larger size, John's feet now felt okay, though he knew it would take time to get used to wearing them again. He handed the smaller size to the shop owner. 'Thanks.'

Ralph handed him an envelope.

'Flight is at ten in the morning, direct to Adelaide then on to Sydney. Dale will pick you up at the airport.'

He handed John the money. 'Ten grand, as ordered. I wish I could be a fly on the wall when you and Jimbo try to book in.'

John stuffed the cash in his pocket. He waved goodbye then left the store. 'Okay Jimbo, time we got pissed at the Darwin Hilton.'

'Na - they won't let a black fella drink in there.'

'Bullshit. Just watch them try while you are with me. Hilton James, and don't spare the horses,' he yelled, taking another smoke from the packet.

The hotel was as plush as John figured it would be, with high pile carpet, a smoker's room and a gaming room. Wait-staff hurried around to meet their customers' every need. A young girl came up.

'Can I help you sir?' she asked.

'Yep, Paul Marsden booked a room for me and my buddy here.' The girl looked at Jimbo, then back at John.

'Mr Marsden, we are not permitted to allow your friend to stay here.' 'Why, because he is black?'

"Company policy sir.'

'Call the manager, please. Now.' John replied tersely.

Hearing the ominous voice, a short-framed man approached. 'Perhaps I can assist you sir.'

'Unless you're the manager, no, you can't.'

'I'm the assistant manager; the manager is away on his meal break.'

'Well then, you will have to do. I have a room booked for me and my friend. Do you have a problem with that?'

The assistant manager avoided eye contact.

'No sir, but our policy is that we don't allow blacks in the bar. However, he is welcome to stay in your room with you.'

'So I have to lock my mate up like a puppy dog because you don't want his black arse on one of your chrome bar stools?'

'No sir – it's just policy.'

'An outdated, provincial policy of gutless racism, correct? Yes, Jim is black, but he bleeds the same colour blood as we do, and if you keep this charade up I am going to splatter that thing you call a nose all over your shitty pimple infested face. Comprende?'

John spun around, addressing the other people in the lobby.

'Anyone here got a problem with my friend James having a beer at the bar with me?' Not a word came from anyone.

'Figured as much, though deep in your guts you say no. Well let me tell you something. This man has fought for his country, even taken a bullet in the guts so you noses-up-in-the-air types can enjoy the Hilton. You got a problem with that, then come and talk to me, Paul Marsden.

Remember that name. Ask for it at the desk if you don't have the guts to come up and have a chat now.'

The manager arrived to the spectacle of this commotion in the lobby. He walked over to the assistant manager.

'In my office now you two' he commanded, pointing also at the young girl.

'Paul and Jimbo, welcome to the Hilton. Room 44 is yours for the night. The items you ordered are in the safe.'

He slipped John the combination.

I've got to take care of these two arse wipes in my office' he grimaced, rolling his eyes and stalking away.

'Don't think I'd like to be in their shoes right now' Jimbo said as he followed John to the lift. 'You laid it on a bit thick about me back there didn't you?'

'Who gives a shit? Got the result I wanted. Now we can have those beers in peace. Bet ya we get freebies all night.'

'Ten bucks we pay.' Jimbo put out his hand. 'Deal! Ugly.'

Room 44 was made up. Two single beds, a private bathroom and a balcony. John found the safe at the bottom of the wardrobe. When he punched in the code, it gave a beep and popped open. He put his hand in and took out two 9mm's with a 13-round clip. He handed one to Jimbo. 'Hope you're carrying your badge?'

'If the cops come, I don't know you Paul.' Jimbo said, placing the pistol under his pillow. 'Are you expecting trouble?'

'No, but Dale called me on the flight in. Someone made a hit on him at the PM's lodge so he figures we'd better be ready in case there's a leak somewhere.'

Jimbo took the pistol from under his pillow, shoved it in his belt and pulled his shirt over it. 'Beer o'clock bro.'

The lounge bar was crowded as they walked in. A lot of faces looked them up and down.

Muttering between groups could be heard. John sat down, offering Jimbo a seat. 'Two of the coldest long beers you've got on tap' he said, placing a fifty on the bar.

The bar tender returned with the drinks. 'On the manager,' he said and stepped back. John swallowed his in two mouthfuls and put his glass back down. 'Same again.'

Once again the barman returned with the drinks and didn't take any money. 'A ten spot I believe sir' said John, holding out his hand to Jimbo.

'Patience, impetuous white man. The night is young. It was for all night, wadjella' Jimbo replied with aplomb.

The now merry men found a table and a menu. John ordered seafood and a lot of it. Jimbo took on one of the house dishes.

'So why has this secret offsider of Dale's been called into play?' Jimbo asked. 'I've got to go to Canberra. It's all I know.'

'But you're not an agent are you?'

'Na, just a person the government forgot existed. That's all.' 'Maybe they're going to un-forget you.'

'I don't think so Jimbo. If they did that, they know they could never serve their country again as politicians.'

'So what Bardi has told me is true?' 'How do you know Bardi?'

'He's my cousin, brother. First cousin, man. We grew up together.'

'Well fuck me. First blackfella I run into is the cousin of one of my best operatives in the field. Hell Jimbo, are you for real?'

'Scout's honour,' Jimbo replied, making the scout's salute with three fingers. 'We just got told you're a VIP fella, that's the long and short of it.'

'Well I am a no-one Jimbo; just a man trying to get his identity back, same as Bardi and the others. Dale reckons he's got the plan to pull it off, so for my men I'm taking the punt and standing up in Canberra; least that's the plan.'

'Sound like Bardi told me the truth about the rock then.' 'Figure you're right Jimbo.'

'Shit! They did a number on you blokes didn't they?'

John put his finger to his mouth; he touched his ears and indicated towards the door. A police officer was looking over the crowd of people eating. He walked straight to John and Jimbo's table.

'Got a call you and your mate've been shit stirring a bit.'

'Who, us? We had a bit of trouble with the assistant manager until the real manager got it sorted. So it's all cool.'

'Well that explains why the assistant manager no longer works here. You two have a good night.' The senior constable turned and walked away.

'Well fuck a duck, thought we might have a shouting match on our hands.'

'He's cool. One of us actually.' Jimbo smiled at John. 'Seems Dale has a lot of your kind around these parts.'

Back at the bar they drank and drank. John was starting to talk left handed Braille, while Jimbo just got the funnies. No one seemed to complain any more. As the hours rolled on, the crowd in the bar decreased. Soon the bartender called last drinks.

CHAPTER SIX

Darwin Airport

Jimbo woke early, rolled out of bed and looked for water. He quickly consumed the jug of cold water from the bar fridge, refilled and replaced it. Then he walked over to where John was still in the land of nod.

'Hey Kelly! Wakey wakey hands of snakey' He stood poking at John.

John opened one eye. 'Fuck... I feel like a bloody dingo's had his way with my mouth. Water! We got water?'

'Ay - whitefella same as blackfella mornin' after.' 'Ten bucks, cobra!' John held out his hand.

'Nothin' wrong with your memory whitey!' Jimbo handed over the note he pulled from his pocket. The drive to the airport took only twenty minutes. On the way over John recalled when he was in Darwin after Cyclone Tracey had wiped the city out. Then he was just a

17- year-old private, waiting for his acceptance to go on the officer training course. He looked up at the large tank on the main drive out. The imprint of a refrigerator that was hurled at by first- time drinkers was still there. John remembered having his photo taken by one of his mates standing next to the tank stand.

Just before the airport entry, he also observed a massive hanger, built to house a B52 bomber.

It was the first time he had noticed it. He figured it was a place he would like to visit one day when he had the time.

Jimbo pulled the taxi to a stop right in front of the QNTAS departure door.

'Well, buddy' said John, 'Time to say good bye. Great night ay? Let's do it again sometime!' Jimbo smiled, perfect white teeth flashing again.

'When you see that cousin brother of mine, give him my love and hey; give him this.' He handed John a roll of notes.

'Where'd ya get that?'

'Last night, when you were pissed out of your tree, I had a little win on the pokies. Invested ten bucks; got back five hundred.'

'Well, if I pull this off, you'll be seeing cousin bro before you know it. Once again, thanks for the night. It's good to let the air out of the tyres once in a while. No better bloke to do it with mate.'

John took his leave, carrying the small travel bag that contained his meagre possessions, and walked towards the reservation clerk at her desk.

'Ticket for Paul Marsden please.'

'I.D. please' the girl asked. This was a question John dreaded.

'Look - I only have one very old expired driver's licence, but it has a photo.' He handed the bent and tattered license over.

The girl looked at the photo then at John. She stood back and took another look. 'I'll just get my supervisor.'

Five minutes later they were back. The supervisor smiled. 'You've been out of circulation for a while?'

'You could say that. Never had the need to have it renewed.'

John's devil-may-care smile was aimed at the man tapping at the computer keyboard. He beckoned the reservation clerk and pointed to the screen.

'When you see the Federal Government as payee with the approval code 616 you don't ask questions. This bloke is travelling on confidential government business.'

She nodded and handed John's licence back.

'I'm sorry if I caused you any inconvenience today sir. You depart from Gate Two, down the walkway and on your right.'

John smiled a Mona Lisa smile in appreciation of Dale's seamless manoeuvring. He had organised everything to prevent any hiccups.

He heard the girl say 'His driver's license said another name; not Marsden. How come you let him go?'

'Like I said, that code says all. It's from ASIO. You never question a 616 code.' 'So he could be a spy

or something?'

'Maybe.' The supervisor walked away.

The departure lounge was crowded with passengers waiting to board. John put his small bag down and picked up a magazine. On the front cover was a picture of Jillian, and the words 'Prime Minister or Proxy PM?'

He flicked to the article, with a cold shiver when he read that people thought Jillian was being manipulated as a proxy PM by her father, David Gillman. He looked back at the photo on the cover. He remembered her face so well. The last night he spent with her before being deployed to the Rock. The letter he got from Jillian three months later informing him he was going to be a father. He closed his eyes for a second and saw her naked beauty lying on the bed.

How he had longed for her these past years. Her father had made damn sure he and his strike team would never see the light of day again as a free citizens.

He opened his eyes when a carrot-topped man sitting next to him commented 'Bloody sexy lady that PM, don't you think?'

John grinned. 'Yeah! Very easy on the eye.' 'I can introduce you to her if you like.'

He had John's attention, though he knew he had to be cautious. 'What - you know her?'

'Kind of. I was on staff with her father when he was in the chair.'

More interested, John pushed a little further. 'So you knew him well then?'

'Wouldn't say well. I was what you'd call his Ops staff officer. Had to oil the wheels, you know. Devise plans; map out the outcomes he wanted and implement them.'

' Interesting!' John extended his hand. 'Sorry, didn't catch your name?' 'Sanderson. Peter Sanderson.' He shook. 'And you are?'

'Paul Marsden. Haven't done nothing as exciting as you have, working for a PM and being a big game player. S'pose you were privy to all the machinations and wheeling and dealing then?' John grinned, hoping his chance companion might forget he had signed the Secrecy Act.

'God yeah' Sanderson replied covertly, enjoying his new-found notoriety. 'All sorts of shit.

If the PM wanted anyone to disappear, I set it up.'

'Dead set? That must have taken a lot of planning. Involved a lot of people. How could you be sure they wouldn't spill their guts somewhere along the line? Always been an interest of mine, you know - the secret squirrel stuff. Would've been a buzz.'

John gave the man a playful nudge. He smiled. John knew he had his confidence. 'Yeah. Sometimes you feel like God. Other times it can be pretty sad actually.' 'Sad? Didn't think spies ever got sad.' John teased.

' Mate - we're human. Sometimes it's not fun - like the time I helped set up a group of soldiers to take a fall on Dev...'

A speaker announced that flight 51 to Sydney was now ready to board. John didn't care. He had what he wanted. 'See you on the flight maybe.'

As John found his seat, he watched to see if the seat next to Sanderson was occupied. Flight attendants were busy making sure things were stored properly and people were in their correct seats. As a mature, full figured attendant leaned across to tend to the needs of a young girl in the window seat, she brushed against him.

John noticed her full breasts and sweet perfume. He stroked his long beard, and the young girl observed

'Must have taken you a long time to grow it that long mister.'

'Yep, sure did. About eighteen years, young 'un,' John replied, smiling. He figured she was not much older than perhaps seven or eight.

'Are you going to Sydney?'

'Yep. Going back to my Mum. Been in Darwin on holidays with my Dad.'

John knew what that meant. Mum and Dad were separated, the kid caught in the middle. He felt a little sad for the child, as he had gone through the same thing. At least his parents were still friends and didn't live that far apart.

'Did you have fun in Darwin?' he asked.

'Sure did! Lots of swimming, and Dad took me to that big museum near the airport. That plane in there is a monster!"

'Really? Well, I've never been there, but everyone says I should go.'

The Captain's voice came over the intercom, advising cabin crew to give the safety brief. It had been a long time since John's last flight in a large aircraft so he paid attention. He even felt under his seat to ensure his life vest was there.

The aircraft was moving slowly backwards. It stopped, and under its own power, began to move down the taxiway. John waited for the rush as full power was added and the speed increased. He could feel the momentum pushing him back in his seat. A small soft hand sought his. Reassuringly, to himself as well as his now slightly panicked companion, he said 'Exciting, isn't it?'

She tried to smile. 'Just don't like that part of flying.'

'Well I don't like the landing, so you'll have to hold my hand when we land.' The smile widened. She gave a gentle squeeze. 'Landing is the fun part.'

John ordered a coffee and asked the young girl if she would like a soft drink.

Eyes wide open. 'Oh yes please, an orange drink would be nice.'

'One coffee and an orange drink please,' he asked the cabin attendant.

He smiled at the new chums and soon returned with the drinks. John sat back, savouring the coffee aroma and observing that his large hands looked ridiculous around the small cup. It felt good to have other people around, even total strangers. In his exile at the bush community, he'd mostly kept to himself, pre-occupied with planning his way back to total freedom. He inwardly seethed at the calculating and merciless set-up that had made him and his team fall guys to the

Prime Minister of the time, ensuring his party's continued funding from America. He often wondered why they hadn't been executed. It would have been simpler. Game over; he would not have to live a double life just to survive. But for Dale and the position he held, they would have been killed. John ached to put his hands around David Gillman's throat and squeeze until the last breath drained from the man's body.

He remembered the set-up well before he was sent to the Rock. How David had provided briefs to make the mission seem of utmost importance to world peace. His aim was getting Bin Ladin to actually sit down with the President of America. The scoop of the millennium.

The yanks on the island made damn sure that was never going to happen. They killed their own President, and then laid the blame on John and his team. Before being sent back, under military arrest, he discovered the real reason.

The Vice President, ambitious for leadership, didn't want talks with Bin Ladin. He wanted total destruction of the Middle Eastern people, and a takeover of the world's remaining fossil fuel reserves. Then they'd be able to manipulate the global market any way they liked. Rockets containing nerve gas, launched from Devils Rock, were to be used. Devils Rock was similar to the training area John used at a place called Indigo near the border point know as Surveyors Corner It was located near the WA, SA and the NT where the boarders met. Indigo was selected because of its remoteness. It had to remain a secret base. For some reason it had mystical powers. Minerals contained in the ground dislike radar signals and later as the space race grew it was discovered that satellite images became very blurred and un-readable.

Bardi one of his team players was borne in the area. He tried to explain about the land. How the elders gave it great respect for its ability to contain secrets. He also told John about the plants that grew in the area. Plants that had great healing power. The Rock was the same. John remembered a geologist had done a lot of testing of the area and had confirmed in his report, that the area was considered a freak of nature. He further reported that in his opinion the only explanation was the planet that hit the Earth and helped form the moon eons ago had in fact struck at Indigo. Results from the impact, Devil's Rock had been formed.

The Rock was actually a chunk of the planet that was hurtled thousands of miles off the coast. This resulted in Indigo being scattered with properties from the planet. Properties not found on any part of earth. Soil and seeds survived the impact and over billions of years had taken hold. The dust particles scattered over Indigo left behind minerals that resisted satellite imaging.

Putting two and two together, John figured the missiles laden with nerve agent would be launched from the Rock to the Middle East. Not another country on the planet could detect the missiles point of origin. One problem – Devil's Rock was British owned. It was a no-go for the yanks to build a fleet base in the Indian Ocean. This one stipulation had cost John everything in the world except his life. He had no identity. Tax records were wiped. Voting enrolments expunged. Medicare deleted.

Anything that could confirm their identity was gone, right down to property ownership and bank accounts. They'd been in a secret holding point guarded by military police in the middle of nowhere for years, until the change of government. Then their guards simply disappeared, leaving them locked in the compound. Now free from the threat of a guard's bullet, they broke the locks and walked out, Unknown reason to John the guards had left vehicles behind in their sudden haste to leave. John and his team took advantage of the unexpected gift. The padlocks on the gates could not withstand the impact form the vehicles and snapped open. On the other side of the fence the feeling of freedom drifted over the men.

John remained focussed. He knew things could change in the tick of a clock. He didn't know why, but it gave him a short advantage. He would need to continue to hide his men. Remote ness was the key. Bardi had arranged for the men to be hidden deep into his tribal lands. His people would take care of the basic needs. John was sent to Jimbo's people. They were a mix of old people, some who'd been trackers and stockmen, others who'd managed to stay out of sight of interfering wadjellas, and a few like Jimbo who'd been taken away but returned with the white man's education. All were managing to live pretty well off the land, as they'd always done.

John knew many of the men wanted to return to family. However, they understood that safety of their brother in arms outweighed the risk. It was going to be a long and painful wait. All agreed to lay low. Scatter themselves among the communities that Jimbo and Bardi knew would hide them. When the all clear was given and only then would they emerge from the secret life they now had to endure for each other. Not matter how long it was going to take.

Their sudden freedom, if you could call it that, didn't last long. Within 18 months the government changed again. David Gillman was back in power. The chase to find John Kelly and his men was back on. They had been in hiding ever since. Only Dale Myers had made sure their location had been kept a secret from Gillman and his henchmen.

John glanced out of the window past the sleeping young girl, at the red desert below. Wild and dangerous country. When training his team, John had learned from the Aboriginals how to respect and live off unforgiving, arid land. John came to love its majesty, learning from its most experienced subjects how to survive and thrive in austerity. This made him the best long range Strike Team Commander the army had ever produced. He had been offered and accepted tribal initiation, which outdid any SAS boot camp, to show his respect for the land and its elders.

The reflection of station homestead rooves flashed far below as the aircraft continued its course to Sydney. He wondered how much the city he hated most of all had changed. It was close to twenty years since he had been in a major city. If Darwin was any indication, he knew Sydney would also be a concrete jungle, a place he was uncomfortable in. Bush skills counted for little in cities. He felt that all his control was gone.

CHAPTER SEVEN

Sydney

The young girl reminded John that the aircraft was coming in to land. She gripped his hand and softly patted it, causing John to grin widely.

'It will be good to sleep in my own bed tonight,' she said, as the wheels of the massive A380 touched down.

John reached for his bag, first passing down the young girl's. After mutual fond goodbyes, she joined the line of people hurrying from the confines of the aircraft. John sat back and waited. He knew he should join soon, as he didn't really want to attract attention.

Eventually he stood up in a gap and shuffled along with the rest of the people, amazed by how many of them dug in their pockets for miniature portable telephones and started punching in codes or talking. He had seen them advertised in an old magazine at Bundy Bundy. John shook his head and continued towards the exit

John heard the sounds of a young boy yelling at his mother 'Look! It's Santa mum! I know cos of his big beard!'

John smiled and called to the lad 'No son, Santa is as white as snow.'

The boy looked disappointed as John hurried to the main doors to avoid the masses of people continually shoving past him and swiping him with trolleys loaded with suitcases, along with the endless lines of people queuing to be served by attendant at the check- in points.

He made it to fresh air, took out a smoke and lit it, only to be told

'You've got to be fifty metres away from the door mister if you want to smoke.'

John paced out fifty metres, sucked hard on the smoke and exhaled it in the direction of the doors.

'Fifty fucking meters' he laughed. 'Hallelujah.'

'World's gone crazy. Can't drink at a bar with a mate, no smoking, what other crazy rules have these people made up?' he said to a fellow smoker standing next to him.

'Not been to the city for a long time ha?" the man asked. 'Many years; many many years.' John replied.

'Well, smokers are now treated like lepers. They hate us.' 'Fuck 'em, I'll stick to my old ways.'

'Not worth the risk man - on the spot fine - $250 bucks. No shit!' the man informed John, squashing his smoke out under his shoe. A woman passing by hissed

'Pick your fucking butt up, loser!'

'See what I mean?' he said, picking it up and flicking it into a sidewalk ashtray.

'Fuck you lady!' yelled John defiantly, flicking his butt onto the road. She shouted at him.

John grinned. 'You want it so much bitch? Go get it!'

The woman spun around, clocked the situation then strode toward him. She whipped out a notepad, flicked it open and wrote up a penalty for littering, thrusting it at John.

'Here, smartarse. Laugh this one off.'

'You got nothing better to do in life then to stand here and watch smokers do the wrong thing? Lady you really need to get a life. You're a sad piece of flesh.'

He dropped the ticket onto the ground and watched as the wind blew it away.

The woman signalled to a police officer, who came over. She explained what had happened and soon John was in handcuffs.

A patrol car pulled close to the curb as Dale stopped his Z plated vehicle and rushed toward the officer. He spoke with him and showed his ASIO badge. John was un-cuffed and handed to Dale.

'Make sure this turkey is kept on a chain' said the cop sourly, walking away. 'Bugger me; a bloke can't even fart now days without getting arrested.'

'A lot of things have changed over the years John. You're in for some big surprises. Come on; let's get you out of this cluster-fuck.'

John laughed. 'Is that what ya call it now-days?' Once in Dale's car, he asked. 'Have any trouble?'

'Na, smooth as silk. Gotta tell ya; that young Jimbo in Darwin is a cracker of a bloke. You know he's related to Bardi?'

'Yes – he's one of my best operatives. No-one suspects a blackfella as an ASIO information officer.'

'So what's all the drama around getting me to this hell-hole?'

'Your freedom I hope, if things turn out right. You'll finally be out of all of this mess. Free to go and do what you want.'

'Still keep in contact with Jillian?' John asked.

'Sure mate. She's as sexy as she was when you last saw her.' 'Does she know I'm alive? How's my son?'

'No, Jillian still thinks you're MIA or KIA. Johnny's doing fine. He's about to graduate from RMC.'

'Jillian got another fella?'

'Nup. She told me she'd never get mixed up in a relationship again. She's always held out hope you might reappear.'

'That's pretty staunch.' Dale looked over.

'John, she cries for you every night. She's still, and always has been, completely in love with you. And no, she doesn't know you're here.'

Dale stopped for traffic lights. John noticed the large green sign pointing to Gulls Flat, the small town where Jillian's father had his farm. Dale swung onto the road.

'Where are you fucking taking me Dale, this is to David's farm!'

'Not to his farm; to our farm I'm hiding you there for now. Jillian'll be out tomorrow.' 'Your place is just across from Gillman's, right?'

'Yep. David's in America on party business, so you won't cross swords with him.' 'Cross swords! I'll kill that excuse for a man. When you find a pub I want to get a carton.' 'Got one! Step ahead of ya mate. It's getting cold in your room.'

'You're a gentleman and a scholar!' John laughed, offering Dale a smoke. 'Can't smoke in this car. Commonwealth vehicle.'

'Fuck 'em.' John lit up and looked for the window winder.

'Use the button on the door - it opens the window.' Dale smiled to himself.

'Struth - you mob are getting really lazy -ya gotta have a little motor to wind the window down. So - what's the upshot of all these covert operations, China?'

Dale kept driving, his eyes fixed on the road.

'Got a job I want you and your team to do. If you play your cards right, you get all you want back.'

'Who do I have to kill?'' John said wearily, flicking the last of the smoke out of the window. Dale laughed. 'I'll explain later. So, how've you been, in general?'

Dale's mobile phone rang. He turned the radio on and started talking into nothing. John was intrigued. The car was Dale's office.

'How'd ya do that?' John laughed.

'Called Blue Tooth. New technology. No big phones anymore John. Everyone has smart phones.'

'Ha! Like those cartoon books I used to read. Calling Dick Tracey!' Dale laughed. He had never seen the funny side of John.

'When Jillian turns up John, promise me you'll wear this bush clobber?'

'Yeah, right mate. I'm not going to win her back dressed like a wino straight off the street.' 'Impact John. Remember, she thinks you're dead. It'll come over a little easier when she puts the pieces together. You know, how you've survived, that kinda thing.'

'Only managed to do that through your cunning; staying a few steps ahead of David and his hangmen.'

'At the moment, Jillian doesn't need to know that. Not if you we are to get your boy and your identity back in one piece.'

Dale looked over at John, who looked stunned. 'You okay with that?'

'I'm not really sure I'll be able to comply with that mate. The boys and I have had near on 20 years off. I haven't seen any of them in close to fifteen. We may not have that much in common now- days. The final word will be up to them. I won't do anything without their backing.'

'So I take it there's no- one else on your team? Just the old squad?'

'No-one. Outsiders are dangerous to us. Don't wanna be watching my back all the time.'

Dale indicated to turn right. He noticed a police car follow and, as it lined up behind him, the blue disco on top lit up.

'Cop. If you've got that 9mm on you, hide the fucker.'

John took it from his bush jacket and placed it under the passenger seat as Dale pulled to the side of the road and waited for the two officers to approach. Dale watched in the rear view. He could see both officers had their side arms drawn.

'Get your weapon. This is going to be an attempted hit.'

John's hand felt the cold steel as he slowly pulled it from under the seat. He flicked the safety off and slipped the weapon under his right hip. He sat quietly as the cop made it to his window.

The police officer motioned for John to step out of the car. John looked at Dale then back at the cop. He slowly put his middle finger in the air. Dale hit the gas pedal and the car shot forward, covering the two cops in a cloud of dust.

'What was that in aid of?' John asked, taking the weapon from under his hip.

'I had an attempt on me a week or so back. Not sure who's ordered the hit but I think it's Gillman. Something to do with a group calling themselves the NWC. I have no idea what it is or what it stands for. Got a bloke in Canberra trying to track 'em down.'

'The New Work Command. Are they still in business? NWC is a yank organisation set up by some of the world's richest people. To get a foot in the door, your nomination fee is a billion dollars, and even that's no guarantee. They intend to take over all the governments of the world - except America's obviously- and impose their rules on all. Failure to follow NWC results in elimination. Total elimination. We are talking the entire population of countries who won't follow. So now you know why America is so hell-bent on protecting Indigo. They help fund it and it's totally secret. Not even America's own space-craft can spy on what's going on. Oh, and don't forget the oil in the Middle East, which will help fund the final program.'

'Fuck, how did you know about Indigo?'

'I learned a lot in the short time I had on Devils Rock. I as an officer was permitted to have newspapers in the Military jail. I asked questions and filed the answers away Dale. Indigo was the second selected site if Devils Rock fell over. This might be of interest to you. If you ever see a small dot tattooed behind a suspect's left ear, he is NWC. More dots, higher they are.

Dale swore again.

'That means David Gillman is high up. He has five dots. I noticed them the other day in Canberra.'

'Five would put him up there as one of the founders. Can't get much higher than that. I'll bet my arse those cops are assassins for NWC.'

'How do you put that into context?'

NWC recruit ex-service men who have seen action. They like special force people mostly, but they'll take any bugger who has been shot at and survived. They've got blokes lining up to enlist - ground soldiers, cops, soldiers, fly boys, navy seals. You name it. Tried to get me before all this shit happened.'

'With membership like that, they've got to have money behind them to pay for it all.' 'Don't you worry about that. NWC has thousands of well-to-do businesses raking in the

funds, and billionaires busting their arses to donate to them on a regular basis.'

Dale pulled to the side again. He got out, opened the boot, took out the shot gun and returned to the driver's seat. 'Just in case.'

John looked it over, extracted one of the shells and examined it. 'Not your normal shotgun round?'

Dale smiled. 'No it's not. It's a high explosive head. Tip a car over with the blast if aimed right.'

'Gotta get me one of these!' John placed the round back into the pump magazine.

The flashing lights appeared again. Dale told John 'They're back' and hit the accelerator.

The Government-issue Ford shot forward as the speedo climbed.

'Dirt road mate!' John said, clambering into the rear seat. 'Hope you're insured 'cos I need to kick the back window out.'

'Can't, it's reinforced.'

John lay on his back as best he could. He kangaroo-kicked the glass with both feet and the window popped out. 'Reinforced! Better get the techo's to look at it.' He swung the shot gun out of the now open window. 'How far does this thing shoot?'

'Two hundred!' Dale yelled. The wind now coming in made it difficult to hear.

John elevated the barrel a little and aimed. He waited until their pursuers were about 250 yards away then fired. Being a very heavy round gave it little range. John could see it fly through the air in an ark then strike the ground. The shot round did the rest. The police car ran over the round just as the High Explosive round exploded. The car leapt into the air and twisted over onto its roof, landing hard on the dirt road.

'Got 'em!' John yelled. 'Stop! I want to check them. May not be ear marked but if they are NWC boys they will be wearing the affiliation ring. Gold with the world map in a stone on it.' Dale slammed on the brakes, skidding to a stop in a cloud of dust, then reversing and gunning the engine. As he made it to the wreck, he swung hard on the steering wheel. The car did a 360 degree turn, again facing their exit road.

'Make it quick! Most likely they've called for backup.'

John got out and ran over to the wreck. The driver's head was hanging out of the side window. He pulled it up and exposed the left ear. No markings but he noticed the ring. Above the ring was what looked like a small skinny wedding ring, he was a supervisor. He made it to the other side. The passenger was still alive. He dragged him from the car and lay him down. He checked his hand, just a ring. 'Ok soldier, who leads you here in Australia?'

The cop spat in John's face.

'Please yourself buddy, be another hour if you called for backup. Given your wounds, I reckon your blood will be all over this gravel road. Hope the NWC got a good 'die on the job policy' if you're married.' John stood up and began to walk away.

'Wait!' He screamed to John.

John came back. 'You've got two minutes. Then I might give you a bit of first aid.' 'David Gillman.'

'Okay buddy, it's your lucky day.' John ran back to the car, took out the first aid kit and began to flush and dress the wounds. Dale arrived and watched on as he patched the fella up with all due care. John finished and turned to Dale. 'You blokes carry morphine?'

'Yep, got a vial in the first aid kit. That's it in the small clear bottle. The syringe should be slipped into the front flap.'

John extracted eight cc and jammed the needle into the dying cop's arm. 'Give you some relief till your buddies arrive, if they get here in the next five minutes.

Fuck it.' John extracted the remaining twenty cc and jammed it into the man's arm. 'Now you'll die on a high.'

Dale sat back in the driver's seat with both hands resting on the steering wheel. He thumped the wheel and spun and faced John. 'I don't bloody get it! Five minutes ago they were going to kill both of us, and then you drag one from the car and give first aid and pain relief. Why?'

'I look at it this way. If I go up against them and get my guts shot out, I would hope as a soldier whoever did it would do the same for me. It's an unwritten code.'

'You Special Forces blokes have some crazy ideas.' Dale started the car and put it into drive. 'So - did he talk?'

'Yep. As we suspected - David. He's Australia's top dog. The five star General. So now are you going to tell me your cunning plan?'

'No, not just you; the whole team. They're all heading to the farm as we speak.' Dale gave a very large grin. 'Oh, and I'll get you one of those surprise shot guns.'

'Better make it half a dozen, with five thousand rounds of the little HE things' John replied, lighting another smoke. 'Oops, window! Forgot the fucking rules.'

'Sounds like you've already agreed to do the mission then?' 'Like I said Dale, depends on the boys.'

John turned and looked out of the side window of the car as the countryside slipped past.

Slowly, some of the landmarks registered in his brain. The old hay-shed; rusting machinery that still stood in the paddock. He remembered that fence posts used to be stacked at the corner of the dirt road. Some were still there. Tall, dead grass had nearly covered them over. 'Not much has changed out this way.' He turned back to the front and half looked in Dale's direction.

'No, and I hope it stays that way. Don't want it to turn into another Sydney or Canberra. It's the place I like to escape to when I feel bogged down with the entire world.'

'How much do you know about a bloke called Peter Sanderson? He used to work for Gillman when all this shit went down.'

Dale shrugged. 'Can't say I know much about him. I was a new kid on the block in those days. I can have him checked out. What am I looking for?'

'Got a feeling he's still very much NWC. I ran into the ranga in Darwin. He let it slip he was one of the masterminds behind Devil's Rock.'

'He didn't recognise you?'

'No fucking idea who he was talking to. Figured I must be some dumb arse who just came in from the bush.' John stroked his copious beard.

'Well, we'll have to keep it that way.' 'How much longer till the farm?'

'Twenty minutes, maybe half an hour.' Dale said, turning onto a very rough gravel road that was in need of grading. John now felt both apprehensive and excited about seeing the men again, and Jillian. He could picture her standing in front of him.

The long road leading to the farm house came into view. Dale turned the vehicle onto the graded drive. Instinctively, he gazed out over the field. It had been something he did as a boy and continued to do every time he made it to the farm.

'Need some rain,' he said to himself.

CHAPTER EIGHT

Gulls Flat. Range View Farm.

Dale stopped the car in front of the familiar, stately two story farm house. John had played at being an "Indiana Jones" type of character there many times.

'Your Mum and Dad still run the place?' John asked, opening the door of the car.

'Mum now, along with my older brother. Dad passed away a few years back. Looks like Sandra and Jillian are here as well.'

Dale pointed to the Ford LTD parked in the open garage.

'I can't go in dressed like this.' John glanced down bemused at the rags he had on.

It was too late. A woman in white slacks and a green blouse appeared at the door of the house, walked to the ballast rail and looked in the direction of Dale's car. She now approached the steps, her eyes fixed on John disbelievingly. She ran towards him.

'John! Oh my God! John, it is you.' She stopped a few paces away. Then her arms went out.

John embraced her. He kissed her head and neck. Her perfume smelt the same as always. "Shrine". It was a brand he had first bought her during their courting days.

She looked into his face. A tear rolled down his cheek and was soon consumed by his large beard. Jillian was crying too. He wiped away the tears and kissed her cheek. 'My God, I didn't think I would ever see you again.'

She snuggled into him. 'Same here.'

Dale stood back, looking. He had not seen the Prime Minister ever look so happy. He walked over to his wife and kissed her. 'It's good to see, don't you think?'

'It is the greatest thing you've done Dale. I'm so happy to see Jillian finally with a smile on her face.' Sandra turned to them. 'Come on you two lovers. I think this calls for a drink.'

John, carrying Jillian over the threshold, stopped at Dale. 'Are the boys here yet?' 'Tomorrow John, they arrive in the morning.' Dale grinned jubilantly as he slapped John's back and walked past him.

The house was well furnished, with a rustic appeal. Dale's mother Nancy had insisted on both brocade and leather lounges, Maxique wood bookcases and lace curtains, now joined by a state of the art flat screen TV, with Foxtel and flat top box

Nancy loved entertaining. She had spent the morning making homemade cakes and biscuits. She happily placed them on a polished, rough timber table that had been cut from the very first tree felled by her grandfather when he started clearing the land. He had been granted the acreage after serving in the First World War.

John remembered Nancy's cooking. When he was a child at the local school, he and Dale would swap lunches. As John's mother made only the normal predictable fare, Dale got the rough end of the deal every time. He eventually woke up and refused to swap.

Jillian sat on John's knee, making it difficult for him to eat and drink, but he didn't care. He was reunited with his lifelong love. That was all that mattered right now. After a while, he rose from the table and said he was going outside to smoke. Jillian followed him. As they both stood on the veranda, John felt his anger return toward her father.

'Do you know why Dale brought me out of hiding?' he asked, looking over the paddocks while leaning on the top rail.

'No. Why? And who cares? We are back together.'

'It matters Jillian. Apparently, I've got to do something to save your government's arse. My gut feeling tells me it has something to do with your father. The end result being his death, or at least being made accountable to both of us and the people of Australia for what he has done and is doing.'

Jillian faced John. 'What are you talking about?'

'It's obvious your father never told you the truth about Devil's Rock - only what he wanted you to know.'

'He told me you and your team were killed in a fight during the guerrilla campaign that was fought on the island. He said you died bravely and if your remains were ever discovered they would be bought back here and given full military honours.'

'He never told you I asked for your hand before I was deployed?' 'No, I found that out from Dale.'

'What about our son? Does he know the truth?'

'I think Dale has explained things to him. I spoke to him on the phone before I left Canberra.

He knows you are alive and wants to meet you.'

'Meet his dead old man. Classic! I missed out on being his father - the footy; cricket; him growing into a young man.' John lit another smoke.

'What happened on Devils?'

'I think Dale is best to brief you on that, along with why he's got me here. I'm going to the guest house to clean up. Shave and look human again, instead of like some old wino out of the gutter, which is how I've been for the past fifteen years, thanks to your old man and the gutless party members he leads.'

John walked away, angry and dejected. Jillian wept.

She had not seen her kind, gentle John like this before. He had changed and she wanted to know why; the whole bloody story, and why he had been kept from her and their son for twenty years.

'I will know the truth my darling. I'll find out everything.'

She watched as John disappeared into the guest house, 500 metres away.

Dale came out and hugged Jillian. 'He wouldn't tell you?' Tearfully, she shook her head. 'God Dale, what happened?'

'Indigo was selected as his team's training area for a reason. No satellite image could be detected on it. Any surveillance just showed as large black spots. You couldn't distinguish anything. We discovered Devils Rock had the same area. That's what the Yanks wanted secrecy. Bin Ladin was waiting on the other side. John was to bring the President to him to discuss a treaty. Bin Ladin only trusted John to be the go between. Once Bin Ladin heard the President was dead, he bolted, knowing the Americans would blame him.

'So the yanks didn't want anyone to know that you knew about the meeting?'

'Not the yanks, PM. David Gillman. It was worth too much to his party. Guaranteed election win. Lose the Yanks and the funding to the party is cut off'

John went to the farm a long time before you got pregnant to ask for your hand, but your dad turned him down flat. His daughter was not marrying a simple army officer. A few months later, John's team was sent to Devils. It was a set-up from the start. The proof is in your father's records, stashed in the shed on his farm. That file, my dear, is something we need to get access to before we ask John and his boys to take a close look at Indigo. I should warn you - if they agree, they'll want a lot in return. Some of it you may not be able to give.'

'Give, after what he and his men have been through? It's the bloody country's damn duty to give! They will be compensated, even if they turn the mission down. No-one deserves what they've been put through. By

God Dale, even if it costs me my job, I'll make sure they get everything they want. Has your office got the ability to deliver?'

'Scratch my back and I'll scratch yours, but we need the file first so I know who the players were at the time, to get them on-side. That is, if they are not NWC operatives.'

'NWC? What the hell is that?' Jillian asked.

'They, my dear, are the mob that set John up. Your father is head of the NWC for Australia.

At least, we're pretty sure he is.'

'I'll do everything in my power Dale. PM's honour.'

'Best you tell John that, not me. He's waiting to hear those words from your own lips.' Dale turned to walk back into the house, stopping near the door. 'He's waiting for you.'

CHAPTER NINE

Range View Farm Guest House

John stood in the bathroom on a carpet of black and grey hair - his newly-shed long beard. Happy now the whiskers were shave-size, he scraped the razor over his foamed jaw. Slowly, the remaining beard fell away, finally exposing the white of his face skin. He didn't hear the guest room door open and close. The shower drowned out the noise.

He stripped naked after he had finished the shave and looked at his reflection. Given what had happened, his once firm and fit body was still in reasonable shape.

Stepping into the shower, John enjoyed the warm water cascading over him. He poured liquid soap onto a wash-cloth and rubbed his tall body, including the appendage which hugged his thigh like a snake resting in a tree branch.

Jillian had entered the guest house and was in the lounge, sipping her wine. With overwhelming emotions of joy, love and gratitude, she rose and undressed. Walking to the shower, she pulled the glass door open and stepped in, hugging John from behind.

'Darling, I've missed you so much.'

John slowly turned to face her. He took her in his arms and kissed her long and tenderly. She responded, running her hands over his body, familiarising herself with its every contour. Her hand reached down to his sleeping serpent. She ran her fingers over the soft shaft until she could feel the blood being pumped into it. Soon it was standing to attention and had grown at least another three inches in her hand. She stroked it gently while still enjoying the rapturous languor of their kisses.

His hands similarly explored the body he had so craved finally cupping the breasts which had nurtured his stolen son. His mouth closed around her obliging nipples, tongue flicking its appreciation of their tumescent response. In a blissful re-enactment of the erotic dance they had so often shared, he sank to his knees, tasting her salty mound, gently separating its petals until his mouth closed around her clitoris. She gasped, every sense flooded with remembrance of past ecstasies, rejoicing that even after such an absence he would unerringly find her triggers. She ached for him, with the anticipation of having him fully inside her.

'Now my darling, now.' She turned her back to him, leaning forward to rest her forehead on her hands on the glass shower screen, and parting her legs.

John cupped her wet, round buttocks in his calloused hands, his penis feeling its way like a heat seeking missile through to the soft, hot, juicy opening awaiting him. As it yielded to his tumescence, he slowly entered, inch by inch. Jillian gave a low scream of pleasure at the long-deprived consolation. He entered more deeply, slowly, reaching around to gently stimulate her clitoris as he slid in and out with mounting exhilaration. She pushed back, gripping him with her vagina, not wanting him to slide out. He held her firmly against him as she writhed toward climax, arching in rapture at his measured, rhythmic penetration. Like well-matched sprinters straining at the tape, Jillian burst through only seconds before he too exploded through the finish line. In the ecstasy of mutual union, they fell into a silent abyss of sheer pleasure; the exhaustion of utter relief.

Jillian reluctantly released him, turning to embrace the ruggedly familiar stranger.

'Ohhh John, my beautiful lost lover. Twenty wasted years. What the hell has my father done?' He pulled her to him and kissed the top of her head.

'Not just him darling – his henchmen as well.'

Dinner was at the main house. Jillian wore a body hugging dress that showed all her attributes. John, in clean jeans and a floral shirt, reckoned she looked eighteen again. Sandra was her immaculate self; hair up, sweeping dinner dress, brooch pinned to bodice. Dale was Dale, not one to over-dress for any occasion. He offered John a beer and led the way to the veranda of the farm house.

Jillian remained inside to help Sandra finish preparing the meal. Sandra looked at Jillian, who radiated the special glow of a woman deeply in love.

'Was it worth the wait?'

Jillian smiled a Mona Lisa smile at her best female friend.

Outside, John lit a smoke, sipped from his beer can and placed it down. He was leaning forward with his elbows resting on his knees.

'I see you've filled Jillian in on some of our exile.'

Dale looked out over the waving tall grass in the paddock. 'Most of it, but you are going to have to tell her the rest.'

'How far did you get?

'Most of Devil's Rock.' Dale explained. 'She really had no idea what her father was up to at the time. How the rest of Australia, in your words, turned its back on you. The struggle after that I don't know too much about, other than my need to keep shielding you from Gillman's people.'

'She agrees to give us the files?'

'Didn't ask her, but given what she knows now, I can't see it being too much of a problem' Dale replied.

John sat back. 'What about her mother?'

Dale shrugged his shoulders; curled his lips. 'No idea.' He stood up and walked back into the house, returning with two fresh cans. As he sat down, John glanced up. Dale's left ear was exposed a little, enough to see three small dots.

John quickly grabbed him and pulled his face close. He twisted his head to ensure he got a very good view behind his ear, then shoved Dale away and spat at him.

'Figured you may've been NWC.'

'Was! As an ASIO junior I was sent in undercover. Worked my way up the ranks so I could attend the high level meetings. David would never discuss anything with anyone below three dots.'

'Bullshit! You're using me to better your own organisation. You're as low as him.'

'Ok - then explain how I kept you hidden and alive. NWC is even now, and will never stop looking for you. The attempted hit was because they've found out who I really am. You can believe it or not John, but that's God's truth.' He handed John the fresh can.

'So obviously - you'd know the NWC inside and out?' John looked over at Dale.

'Yes, I even got on the decision making council. That's when I took over your project. I could see what they were going to do. That bloke Peter Sanderson, he's still NWC, directly under David. I'd say he recognised you mate.'

'Why do you say that?'

'Intercepted an e-mail message to David, "Found John"; hence the attempted hit.' 'So this place is not all that safe?'

'No. You need Jillian to get her mother over here so you and I can find those files. John, my gut tells me we're running out of time. We've got to act now.'

'We! There's no "we" anymore Dale. I'm past it. Forget "us, we and all for your country!" My men feel the same.'

'What about your officer's oath?'

'Trust and loyalty? Come on mate! This nation is

surviving on lies. I might've been out of circulation for a long time, but I'm not blind to what's going on Dale. You want me to be loyal to a nation that's done this to me and my team?'

'Point taken, but what about your son and Jillian? Young John should at least know the truth.

He deserves that much.'

John turned and looked at Dale. 'I don't even know my son, why should I care?'

'Because he's blood. He has your genes running through his body. And like you, he's a direct relative of the infamous Ned Kelly! Poor barstard'd turn in his grave if he thought his great- great- great- grandson'd turned his back on a nation in need.'

John laughed. 'Ned was nothing but a two bit robber and murderer who'd kill you for the shirt on your back.'

'Perhaps John, but he lived by a code, not much different from your own. He wanted freedom for all; land to offer disadvantaged people, away from political leaders who drained 'em dry with taxes and unfair laws. I remember you saying that once. Your own Utopia, remember that? This is the biggest chance you'll ever have of achieving it.'

'Tell ya what Dale; Utopia is part of the deal. I know of two cattle stations close to Indigo.

You get me the deeds to them, along with a few other things, and I might re-consider.' 'Why near Indigo?

'Because one of my men has the spiritual rights to the

area. He knows its secrets and its pitfalls. I also want Doc back, you remember Doc?'

'I do. Might be a bit hard. He's graduated med school and has a thriving practice in Perth. He might not want to walk away from that.'

'He will when he finds out it's for the boys. At least he's held firm to our beliefs.'

Dale laughed out loud. 'How do I know if I set this up you won't go cold on me re Indigo?'

'It's a risk Dale. We all take 'em. Besides, I'm not having a bunch of Yanks living next to my Utopia; no way!

Dale put out his hand. 'Deal! I'll get the ball rolling.' John accepted it. 'Let's eat.'

Roast lamb was on offer. John was excited. It had been many years since he had relished the succulent, tender meat of lamb. It accompanied some of his happiest memories, from his mother's Sunday roast in childhood to happier times with Jillian. He dug in; plenty of veggies and a pile of meat with rich gravy spread over the offerings. He accepted the glass of wine, smiled at Jillian and gave her a wink. Like a young love-struck girl, she blushed.

'Well my darling, Dale has something to tell you. I'm off to have a shower. See you at the cottage.' He took his leave.

CHAPTER TEN

Gillman's Farm – The Shed

Darkness fell over the land. John could just make out the shapes of the buildings. A soft light shone from the farm house. He hoped the sheep dog would not alert the occupants that he was where he should not be.

He took the long way around, past the hay shed to the side, and found the larger shed that was built into the mud-brick hut. He tried the door. It was locked. Gently, he placed the remains of a steel picket into a chain that was wrapped around the openings in the door frame, and applied pressure. The bolt holding the chain gave way and the door opened.

As he eased his body inside, into the darkness, and pulled the door closed behind him, one of the dogs barked. John froze, looking in the direction of the house out of the small opening that the chain was threaded through. Nothing appeared to stir. Quietly he found his lighter in his pocket and flicked it till a small flame illuminated the interior of the shed.

He felt over the rafters, as he was sure this was where David hid the key to the mud brick cottage. His fingers found the small object. Inserting it in the keyhole, he heard footsteps. The light died as he prepared to stand and fight. He listened again, and then laughed a little, recognising that it was the milking cow stumbling around in the pen to the side of the shed.

The door opened without too much of a problem. Standing in the room, his lighter revealed lines of meticulously labelled filing cabinets. He stooped to investigate further, then found what he was looking for. Devils Rock. The second drawer was named Kelly Strike Team Delta. He pulled at the drawer; it was locked. His pocket knife soon opened the cheap lock that guarded a man's secrets, secrets David Gilman hoped would never be revealed. He took out the row of files.

He had no time to sit and read them. The cabinet next to it was titled Indigo. Once again he took care of the lock and removed the files. An empty plastic waste bin proved handy – John placed his bounty inside and left the hut the same way he had arrived.

When he got back to the guest quarters, Jillian was still in the main house. John laid the files out in military fashion in the spare room and began to read them, taking mental notes. He felt the hair on the back of his neck tighten as he read. They painted a very clear picture of the whole damn operation on Devils, the winners and losers. He was the loser.

Names popped out of the file. Written notes to the side of the typed pages indicated who had read the documents. It was army protocol - initialling comments to indicate they had been read.

Hearing a noise, he quickly placed the files back into the bin and shoved them under the spare bed, making sure the quilt reached the floor to conceal them. He hurried to the kitchen, grabbed a magazine and pretended to be reading it when Dale and Jillian walked in.

Jillian carried a glass of wine. She appeared to have had a few in the interim. She flicked her shoes off and sat down on one of the chairs.

'So! What's up lover? Ready for another ambush?'

John gave a small grin. He had never seen her tipsy, let alone drunk. She was funny. He wondered how she was going to feel in the morning, but it was good to see her letting her hair down. Her father always maintained that she was a lady who should remember what family she belonged to.

Dale came over. 'We got the all clear to get the files.'

'Already done Dale. They're in the lounge room. We can go over them in the morning. I got to get this lady to bed before she changes her mind.'

Dale laughed and said good night. 'Can I take the files with me?'

'Nope, not till I have read them. Had too many secrets kept from me, and at the moment I don't know who to believe.'

'Come on lover, to bed!' demanded Jillian, slurring her words.

'I think I'd better leave.' Dale smiled and quietly backed out of the room.

John turned his attention to a very drunk PM. 'Better get you into bed.' He scooped her up in his arms; the wine glass fell to the floor and smashed. She was asleep in his arms as he carried her to the master bedroom and lay her down. He began to undress her. He took his time savouring every view of her naked body as he slowly unwrapped it from her clothing. She was as toned as he remembered her at eighteen, when one night at the drive-in she allowed him to take her virginity.

He covered her over, dimmed the light, then walked to the kitchen, took a beer and went to the spare bedroom. He emptied the bin, spread out the files, sat on the bed and began to read.

He looked at the dozen empty cans on the floor, then at his wrist watch. It was four thirty in the morning. Dale was telling the truth. David had suspected him to be a plant many years back, but never had the information to take it to the elders and have the matter dealt with. John and his team remained marked men. 'Shoot on sight, no question' was the order signed by David and the executive members of NWC.

John put the last file down and sobbed. He could not believe that David Gilman and his party would lower themselves to such a scam only to remain in power. From what he could see in the files, Jillian was ignorant of her father's ruthless machinations.

He made it to the bedroom. Jillian was asleep, until he crawled into the bed. She woke and climbed gently on top of him. 'Make love to me John.'

Morning arrived; the sun began to shine through the window and into his eyes. Jillian was still next to him, naked. He eased himself out of bed and ventured into the kitchen. Finding eggs and bacon in the fridge, he began to cook breakfast. He was relieved that Dale was not involved, and that Jillian apparently had no idea of the actions of her father and his team of cut-throats who had once governed the country. He had confirmation in writing of what he had always known – that David manipulated Jillian's thinking toward taking the role of PM so he could pull the strings from the side.

He found a large tin tray and dished up a hearty breakfast, then dashed outside, picked a single red rose, and put it in a small Vegemite jar on the side. He picked it up and walked whistling into the bedroom. 'Room service darling, wake up.'

Slowly her eyes opened and she sat up in bed, smiling she fluffed his pillow and made it into a steady platform for the tray to rest on.

'Sleep well?' she asked.

'This is the way I want to spend the rest of my days with you Jillian.'

'Is that a proposal? If it is, then the answer is yes. This time you don't have to ask dear old Dad.'

'It is, and when I get this all sorted, I am going to take you to my Utopia. You and our son.'

'Dale mentioned something about that. I think this country owes you and your men that much. I'm going to call my office today and have my most trusted advisor make it happen. I'm also going to get your identities reinstated; including the back pay you're all owed. Dale is going to make that happen.'

CHAPTER ELEVEN

The Choppers Arrive

The titanic thumping of large rotor blades heralded the arrival of three large Chinooks, which slowly set down near the shearing quarters. John leapt up and ran outside. The boys were here.

Running toward the choppers, he saw the men exiting one of them, and counted them off. All ten were there. The two other helicopters discharged their loads of 4X4 vehicles, machine guns and 50 calibre sniper rifles. John had not noticed Dale was standing next to him.

'The shot guns you wanted will be here this arvo.'
'Man of your word' John said.

He noticed the men lining up. Roo stood in front. His Sergeant Major voice had not changed as he called the men to attention. He then turned and faced John. Shouting, he announced 'Delta team ready for your inspection sir.'

John Kelly walked over and stopped in front of Roo, as if to return his salute. Instead he grabbed the man and hugged him.

'It's so good to see you brother.'

Roo was what they called a career man. He had made Warrant Officer, Class One, in ten short years of service. There wasn't a weapon the man had not used and his field craft was second to none. He had fought all over the "hot spots", and been wounded a few times, but had never forgotten his own code, "Give All." This he had carried with him in his training of Delta. Roo was the man the strike team looked to for discipline - usually a swiftly administered thump behind the ear, out of sight of the rest of the men. John was yet to meet a man who could put Roo on his arse.

Walking over to the line of troops, John stopped in front of every man, hugged and then talked to him. To Bardi, who was Aboriginal and one of the finest soldiers John had served with, he enquired

'How's the leg?'

'Got the plaster off two days ago Feel like I could do twenty miles!

At the end of the line he stopped at Doc, dressed as if he was about to go to work in his surgery.

'Didn't think you would let me down Doc. Welcome home.'

'Just hope my secretary cancels the operations list for today. But I do have to go back and tidy things up'

Jillian stood at the door of the cottage, moved almost to tears as she proudly watched John. She began to understand how these eleven men had formed such a strong bond; one that could never be broken.

'Got Frazer Station for you boys to train. Your equipment will be dropped off with you. You leave tomorrow' Dale explained.

'The boys haven't voted yet,' John reminded him, the

damning contents of the files still fresh in his mind. 'Give us an hour to discuss it. You'd best have good news about the other part of the deal – all of it' John reminded him audibly enough for his men to overhear.

'Have to involve the PM and her Party on that one.'

'Then do it. Now. The deal is off if we've got no word in an hour.' 'You're getting a bit pushy John?'

'I said from the start - no firm deal - no deal at all. Seems the ball's in my court at the moment Dale. It's a nice change.'

Dale nodded. He walked over and spoke to the load-master of the two transport choppers - well out of earshot. Eventually he nodded, then walked to the house.

'Got a deal to make!' he shouted to John.

Jillian came over, and John introduced her to the men. 'Have you put it to them yet?' she asked him. 'No, not till the deal is water-tight.'

'My part is done. What's the hold up?' she asked.

'Best you ask Dale. He seems to be stalling. Got a bad feeling about that.' He kissed Jillian. 'I've got to check something out. Back in a minute.'

He ran back and grabbed one of the files, then replaced it, Something Bardi said about "magic mud" took John's mind back instantly to an article he had merely skimmed over. He found the page, pulled it from the file, folded it and tucked it into his shirt pocket, along with the geologist's report on the Indigo and

Devil's Rock area, which he also pocketed.

He walked back to Jillian.

'You sure about your end of the deal?' 'Of course - it affects us as well.'

'Okay, you're on. Don't tell Dale at this point. Me and the lads are going to leave as soon as the fly-boys have refuelled these grinders. Confirm that to the flight captain in the lead aircraft? He won't say no to the PM.'

'And me John? What should I do?'

'Best you're on the lead chopper with me.'

Dale returned both thumbs up. 'Done deal! Two stations, Frazer and Charlie's Hut.' 'Our ID's and the rest?' John asked.

'Being processed now, will take a little time. Your back pay – all 20 years' worth - will be sent out to Frazer in cash, along with all the necessary papers.'

'Just in time, we head off in 25 minutes' John said. 'You can tell Canberra the PM is on an extended holiday.'

'Why so early - leaving I mean?' asked Dale, startled at the rapid turn of events. 'We like to surprise our enemy.' John winked at Dale.

'Load em up Roo!' John gave the order and soon the men were reboarding the choppers. 'I'll brief you in flight.'

The Chinooks lifted off, sending dust clouds into the

air. Their noses dipped a little as the pilots bought them on track for the flight. The engines roared as power was added. Soon the three hulking machines seemed nothing more than dragonflies in the blue sky over the farm.

John saw the ground and landmarks getting smaller as height was gained. At correct altitude the engines hummed, making it possible to be heard. John called for their attention. He was not sure how he was going to tell them this was their final mission, that after this they were free agents. Everything they'd lost would be restored. John told them what he knew about NWC, then settled back, held Jillian's hand and closed his eyes. Sleep triumphed over the noise of the chopper as he dreamt of better things. Utopia was top of his list.

CHAPTER TWELVE

Hawker, South Australia

Townspeople gathered as the great birds settled on the local football oval. It was not uncommon to see military aircraft and personnel visit the small outstation. The pilot announced they would be on the ground for an hour while refuelling. A bus would take them into town to get any last minute supplies.

A female onlooker saw Jillian walk with John to the bus, and soon the rumours were out. The Prime Minister was in their town.   Jillian's every move and purchase was soon spread abroad by many "two-legged reporters". When John bought some lacy lingerie for her at the local all-in- one store, the older man at the till didn't blink an eye.

'Ammo - you sell it here?'

The man pointed to the rack at the side of the shop.

John nodded; then walked over and checked out the range of weapons. He selected three long barrel shot guns, two 22 hornet's, scopes and five thirty-o-six rifles.

He murmured to Jillian 'Gotta pull a fast one here. Need your help.'

Addressing the storeman, he said 'We'll take the lot thanks, plus all the ammo you have in stock.'

'Hope you've got permits mister. No gun walks out of my store without one.'

Jillian had followed John to the counter. She beckoned the shop assistant aside and they spoke in low voices. John could see him nodding. She looked back.

'Pay him. He'll have it all delivered to the choppers.'

John nodded his thanks and walked outside. 'Anything you need?'

'A cold drink,' she replied, looking at the soft drink machine standing on the dusty veranda.

Equipment loaded and aircraft refuelled, the pilot ordered the team to board and strap in. The Chinooks climbed into the air and John noticed the Load Sergeant from the third chopper had taken a seat on theirs. He was the one that Dale had spoken to at the farm.

The sergeant made his way to John, and grinned as he sat down. 'You blokes on some secret training mission?'

'Could say that' John replied.

'Bit weird eh, the guy back at the farm organising all this equipment for you fellas to train with? He told me to remove these from the sniper rifles.' He handed John a firing bolt from one of the rifles.

John turned and faced him. 'It's a safety thing Sergeant?'

'Yep, and I noticed the rounds have been tampered with too. I looked at one of them. Seems half the powder charge has been removed. Be lucky if the bullet got all the way down the barrel.'

John tried to glance at the man's ear; there were no dots he could see.

'If I were you I'd put down a couple of hundred clicks from the final destination and drive in.

You know; then you have the element of surprise.' 'OK, who are you really? John asked.

Handing over his ID badge, he replied 'Captain Brian Thomas, defence security. I got a red flag when this mission was not approved via the right channels. I get edgy when ASIO puts their nose into military business. So I played along and joined the flight team disguised as a flight Sergeant. Besides, we've had our eye on Myers for a long time. He's done some really wacky stuff, hiding a bunch of soldiers, who were arrested for something on Devil's Rock, his dealings with old man Gillman. He's up to something but we have no idea what it is.'

'Well Captain, you're looking at the soldiers from Devils.'

'Figured you might be. I was a load master on the flight that bought you all back to Australia.

Can you tell me what happened after you returned?'

'Yep – twenty years of hell. Lost ID's; couldn't even open a bank account, let alone make money. Went bush for 15 years, in hiding with desert blacks. Myers kept our secret we thought.'

'Yeah – he didn't let on, but the Defence Secretary knew all along where you all were. We set up the guard's disappearance hoping it would expose who was pulling the strings in ASIO. It was my department's idea to set up Devil's. We had to expose the then PM, ASIO and a mob calling 'emselves NWC. We reckon Indigo was chosen so our own country couldn't satellite what was going on. DEFSEC know about the President's mission, and we believe Indigo is the second attempt on the Middle East. Sorry Sir for what we did. If it's any consolation, I have all your men ID's and bank accounts with 20 years' back pay in the second chopper. By the way, you should be wearing these.'

He handed John a set of Major flashes.

'You were never discharged from the army, because we figured we'd need your team at some point in time. On behalf of a grateful nation I apologise for all that was done, though I know that's small consolation - it can never give you back those years. I'll brief the PM about the whole nine yards and Sir - I will tell all.'

The captain began to stand up. John gripped his arm.

'I want you on this mission as my Intel officer. I'd also like you to arrange that my son join us after his graduation. His mum's missing him and - there's nothing worse than PMT!"

The Captain winked at John.

'You and the PM, man I would have never figured that out in a million years.'

He got up, politely requested that Jillian join him in an unoccupied area, and took out his briefcase.

John scanned his maps. He knew exactly where he wanted to set down and make their headquarters. It was only fifty kilometres from Frazer's Station. He leant over and spoke to Dicko.

'You get all that computer stuff you asked for?'

Dicko tapped the large army store bag. 'And more Sir.' 'Satellite ready?'

'Yep! Got a model not even yet released! Can hack into anything with this.'

'Pass it around. We're going to set down near Charlies hut and drive to Frazer's. Each of you is assigned his particular filed of expertise.'

'Fuck! That means Bardi's the cook again! Shit. Snake and lizard on the menu.' John walked to the cockpit and tapped the pilot. He pointed to the mark at Charlie's Hut.

'Drop-point has changed, and I'm taking your load sergeant with us.' The pilot nodded. 'I'll let the other aircraft know.'

John leaned forward. 'Not by the radio, hey. Use the telex machine you blokes carry up here.'

John got back to the rear, sat down near Roo and briefed him. Roo simply nodded, and a few moments later had the men in a welter of activity, checking and rechecking their gear, confirming one at a time with the thumbs up. They were motley looking bunch with their Beards and tattered clothing. Most wore rubber thongs as shoes.

'You got all the shit I asked the PM to order?' John asked the Captain.

'And a few that weren't requested but might come in handy.' He smiled at John. 'Seems the PM is on board with what's going on. She insists that Myer's wife is out of bounds.'

'Done deal,' John replied, helping Jillian up and walking with her back to their seats. He felt in control for the first time in many years. It was good to be with his crack team and this time, calling the shots.

CHAPTER THIRTEEN

Charlie's Hut - Deep in the South Australian Outback

The green jump-light came on in the back of the aircraft. It was the signal the men had waited for. Soon they would be on terra firma and in control, doing what they did best. 'Absolute silence on landing' Roo yelled the instruction. 'We've got 15 minutes on touchdown to get all the gear out. Can't risk 'em havin' some kinda radar that'll tell 'em where we are. Bardi, you're driving the boss's vehicle. Rat, Boomer, Adder; you're in the second. Fletch, me and Paterson' have got number three, the rest in four. We mount the fifty calibres before departure. When we get to the high ridge on the northern part, test-fire your weapons. Each man is to carry his own sniper rifle.'

All members of Strike Team Delta nodded that they understood the orders.

'Okay everyone, stand up!' Roo barked, as the lead chopper hovered just above the ground to make its touchdown. As soon as the rear door was lowered, the men one at a time exited and ran toward the other two, preparing to take control of the equipment.

The choppers landed and the rotors stayed spinning; the pilot knew what a hot drop was. The driver assigned to the vehicles ran to the rear and soon the five Landcruisers were out.

Captain Thomas ran into the rear of chopper three, grabbed the weapon container and exited swiftly, handing the firing bolts to the gun operators. Each weapon was placed on mounts and bolts inserted. The gun operators clicked in two hundred-round belts and pulled the cocking levers to the rear. Once satisfied, each man raised his right hand to indicate the weapons were "hot."

Roo halted his stop watch. 'Twelve minutes!' he yelled. 'Well done. We move in three.' The column of five vehicles took off in a northerly direction. Each had a gun operator standing behind each weapon mounted on the back of the utes. The remaining equipment was tied down on the rear trays to stop it from bouncing off on the rough, ungraded roads. John had his map open, resting across both his knees and Jillian's. His hand stroked her thigh under the map, and she moved closer in response.

'High ridge in three' John said to the gun operator on the back. Dicko spun the weapon. He aimed it at the target, a pile of rock about five hundred metres away, and squeezed down on the firing lever. The gun jumped but that was all. Dicko looked at the target; nothing had hit it. He banged on the roof and Bardi pulled to a stop, as did the other vehicles.

Dicko had been a fifty cal man all his service life. He knew the weapon inside out. He pulled back the bolt and swore as he looked down the barrel. The head of the round was jammed half way down. It was something he had never seen before.

'We've got a problem Boss,' he said, as John got out of the cab. 'Seems we only got half load rounds.'

John took an unfired round from the belt. He got the ute pliers out of a small tool kit and removed the head, then looked into the brass casing and poured the powder onto his hands. 'Half load alright. Roo - check the rest of the ammo. Bardi, we stay here tonight. We're not moving till we sort this problem. Captain, you got any ideas?'

Captain Thomas looked at the delivery papers. They would tell him what weapons store the ammo came from. 'Bloody hell, Minister of Defence ordered this batch.'

'Roo, dump the jammed 50 cal but not the ammo. No bloody good having them with a fucking lump of lead stuck down the barrel.'

'Hey boss – what say we take the other three that haven't fired yet and reload the ammo when we get to Frazer's? At least we'll have guns with a bit of hitting power then.'

'Do it!' John barked. 'Check the launchers as well, and all the other weapons. Tell the boys we're now on Orange Alert at all times.'

'You heard, Adder,' relayed Roo. 'Get the security organised.'

Bardi soon had the shelter up and had posted "Ladies right, Blokes left". Pointing to the sign, Jillian asked 'What's that about?'

'Toilets dear. Shovel and dunny paper hanging on the tree over there.' John pointed. Adder put out the sensor fence and placed the lead into the control box.

'Out at one hundred!' he shouted so all could hear.

'Explain John!' Jillian asked, perplexed at the rapid-fire and mostly incomprehensible army jargon flying about.

'Security laser fence. It's out at one hundred metres. Don't go past it or you could be filled with little lead objects.'

'Oh. Then guess who's escorting me to the toilet?' Jillian grinned.

Bardi prepared a meal, using what was available from a ten man ration pack. He emptied their contents into the pot and heated a "stew." Tinned steak and kidney pie mixed with potatoes, peas and sweet corn, as well as the assorted contents of other cans in the ration pack. Jillian watched with interest. The tins that were emptied into the pot stood in line. Once the stew was hot, Bardi scooped it back into the empty tins, except one portion, served on the only plate Jillian could see.

'Grub's up,' Bardi announced.

The men took one tin each, then returned to find a seat on the rocky outcrop. John picked up his tin and carried the plate to Jillian. She took it, walked back to the pot and scooped the contents of her plate back into one of the empty tins. With a wry smile at her companions, she took her spoon and began to eat.

All eyes had followed this episode, the men initially suspecting the PM was demonstrating that the food on offer was not to her standard. When she ate from a tin like the rest of them, they mostly concealed their amusement, though a grin or two was apparent.

'Actually Bardi, this is not too foul! Might have to get the recipe'

'It's classified I'm afraid - a closely guarded secret. If I unscrambled the recipe, I'd have to kill you. Oh ok - just chuck it all together and hope for the best.' Bardi giggled, his white teeth glowing against dark lips.

Rat and Fletch had first watch. They perched themselves high on an outcrop that gave a commanding view over both their campsite and along the road leading to and away from it.

Rat estimated outward to five hundred meters, as that range was his best target acquisition. He mentally marked the points around the periphery, ensuring his reaction time. His firing point was simple; a boulder provided cover, and he had prepared six magazines of ammo within easy reach for a smooth and rapid change-over. He dripped a little gun oil onto the working parts of the weapon's bolt and chamber area, then fine-tuned its sight and finally, double-checked his battery pack to ensure an easy changeover to night vision. Happy now, he fished a high protein bar from his 24 hour pack and chewed it with relish.

To his front was wild country, flat ground that suddenly morphed into large rock formations.

On the flat ground, termite nests dominated. Some were as tall as a man. A wide, dry river-bed ran to the east. Rat scanned it with the times-22 sight on his sniper rifle, studiously checking anything that looked remotely like it should not be there. Once sure no threat was posed, he moved on to the next possible ambush. He knew Fletch was doing exactly the same on all obvious entry points.

Pointing, he said 'Fletch! Scan that ridge to the north-east. I think I got a flash – could've been a windscreen.'

Fletch complied, taking a long time to carry out the task. He stopped his scan, then swung his rifle-sights back to the leading edge of a group of trees. An obscure shape was causing him concern. 'Something there mate; don't quite know what it is.'

Rat aimed a Long Range View and heat detector. Sensors told him there was a heat variation at the target. He cranked the focal image 60 times closer.

'Got a hit Fletch. Two blokes and a vehicle.'

He shot the range finder laser to the area. Within seconds its echo returned and "Distance to Target" was displayed on-screen. 'Three thousand,' he announced.

'Get John' commanded Fletch softly, not a hint of panic in his voice. John swiftly appeared and looked through the range finder.

'Maybe it's two stockmen. I'll send a probe team out to get a closer look.'

On his return to the camp, John stopped. His eye caught a flash of light from the direction the boys were concerned about. Crouching, he peered at the small clump of bushes through field binoculars which lacked the power to materialise a solution. One thing he knew - whoever was down there didn't care that others knew. He made out the flames of a fire.

John stood and began to walk back down the ridge to the flat ground where they had set up camp. As he turned the corner, near a small rocky outcrop, his body was suddenly slammed against the rocks. He tried to fight back against whatever it was that had suddenly attacked.

'Roo! What the fuck are you doing?' he asked, as his unlikely assailants grip was released and John was able to breathe again.

Roo pointed. An American Apache attack helicopter was hovering near the dry river bed.

John could see pods of weapons fixed to the side. At the front was the dreaded thirty millimetre Gatling gun with a firing rate of 20,000 rounds per minute.

'What the fuck is that doing out here?'

'Looking for us?' Roo ventured, now with his thirty-o-six rifle pointed in the chopper's direction. He no longer trusted the weapons issued to them.

'It's getting spooky I admit. Our vehicles, are they under cam nets?'

'Yep, fastest I've seen the boys move in ages. Heard the beat coming miles out. Before I locked eyes on it, the nets were up and the men under cover' Roo declared, looking at the chopper.

'Go back, get a probe team and have 'em check out those people in the bushes,' commanded John, jerking his thumb toward the still mysterious destination.

Roo kept low, slid down the rocks and was soon engulfed in the surrounds. He made the camp and quickly had Boomer and Paterson decked out. He watched the two men hugging the rocks on their way to the target area.

Jillian approached Roo. 'What's going on?'

'Not sure Prime Minister, but that chopper up there is not Australian and John saw two people in the bushes about three clicks away. Getting it checked out. You better get back under the nets.' He held the side of a net draped over one of the utes. Reluctantly, she obeyed.

Spider had been sitting near a tree with his rifle over his lap, but when alerted with hand gestures, was soon standing near Roo. The two men walked off purposefully, quickly melting into the forbidding landscape.

CHAPTER FOURTEEN

Camp Site

Spider, who was in the lead continued to stop every hundred metres, take cover and scan the distant ground before moving on again. He could now smell the smoke coming from the fire.

Doing a Leapfrog manoeuvre Roo watched for the all clear before moving to Spider's position. This continued all the way in.

Paterson and Boomer kept low in the river bed. Boomer considered it too open, so he instructed Paterson to walk under cover of the tree line that followed the white sand.

With Roo and Spider in sight they moved silently towards their target.

Roo was now only meters away from two men sitting on camp stretchers near the fire. He turned to his right and signalled Spider.

Spider snuck in closer as he watched Paterson and Boomer take up cover positions. The trap was set and ready to spring when suddenly the thumping of rotors scattered the few birds resting in the trees. Without warning, the deadly thirty mm cannon at the front of the chopper opened up. The aim was true; the two men at the fire were blasted in what looked like a sheet of fire, the remains of their bodies riddled. Both fell from the stretchers, one face down in the fire. Roo knew he would have been dead from the first round that had found its target.

Pushing closer to what cover he had, Spider saw Roo give the signal to just observe what was going on. Four men descended from the chopper on repelling lines, dressed in American Special Forces field cam gear. All carried M16 field issue rifles.

The tallest of the four made it to the fire. He checked the kill then, walking to the vehicle, began to pull things out, looking for something. Something worth killing two people in cold blood for.

Spider saw the man who appeared to be the team leader tuck maps and papers into his field jacket. The other three looked about furtively, covering him. Boomer aimed his rifle at the pilot of the chopper. He waited for Crow to confirm he had the co-pilot in sight. The small transmitter spoke softly in his ear, 'target two confirmed – I have clear shot.'

Boomer called it in, Roo listened. 'T1 and 2 in sights; you got two on left of vehicle and other two near fire. Spider your fire, Roo your vehicle. Acquire and fire in 10 seconds.'

Ten seconds passed. Suddenly the chopper dipped forward, rolled onto its back and beat itself to death. Blood splatters from both pilots stained the cockpit glass red with brains and blood.

Spider took out his targets with two quick squeezes of the trigger. At the same time Roo dispatched both men near the vehicle. Silence fell over the small clump of bush. Roo moved forward, his rifle still at the ready, waving it first over the two at the fire, then at the vehicle. Nothing moved. All head shots had ensured a clean kill. Roo took whatever it was the U.S. Ranger Captain had stuffed in his field jacket. He didn't bother looking at the papers.

By the time he and his team made it back to the camp, Rat, Fletch and the remainder of the Strike Force were already there. John was tending to a wound in Bardi's leg. Instantly Roo knew it was a gunshot wound.

John looked at Roo. 'Get the boys ready, they have Jillian.' 'Who, how many?' Roo asked.

'Three best I could make out. Must've dropped 'em by rope behind the ridge. While we were dispatching the others they sprang their trap.' He threw down the wrapping of the field dressing. 'And we fell for it.'

Captain Thomas staggered towards Adder. He was holding his guts, blood oozing from the wound. The blood was mixed in with faeces from his bowel. Adder reached out and grabbed him, trying to prevent his fall. Too late. The Captain rolled over, grunted, and then died.

Roo handed John the maps and papers. 'One thing's got me beat. They knew where we were.'

'Yep, beginning to wonder about that myself. Bring her back to me Roo, alive.'

Roo nodded and turned to the men. 'We do a four-ways leap, microphones on. Sniper control is Boomer. Paterson you're my side man.' He turned to face John and said meaningly 'We'll find 'er mate.'

The men set off. John went back over to Bardi, who was propped against the wheel of one of the vehicles. 'How's it going mate?'

'Wish to fuck Doc was here. You don't make a good nurse.' He smiled, then instantly sobered. "Boss, this is bad country. Unless you know what you're doing out there, you die.'

'This is not your country though Bardi' John said.

'No but it neighbours mine. See those big hills over there?' he pointed. 'My land starts the other side of them.'

'So we're not that far from Frazer's?'

'Fifty clicks north over that hill. Indigo is about seventy away.' Bardi tried to move his leg a little. 'Put a splint on me Boss and I'll take you to 'em.'

'We've got no bloody idea where they've gone.'

'Boss, I know this country as well as you'd know your way around your home town. The secret waterholes, the cave systems and how to find tucker. There are no B rations in this area. Our training area is not for another seventy clicks.'

'You rest for a while Bardi. Got to allow your body to get its blood supply back in order.

Trying to walk on that leg will open the wound further and you'll bleed out on me. No, we stay put for now.'

'Ok, but do me a favour. Go down to the river. You'll find a little pink and purple plant. Get three of 'em with the roots still on and bring 'em back to me. Must have the roots Boss', Bardi said, still sounding like the ever-loyal soldier he was.

John picked up one of the shotguns. 'Be ten minutes.' John didn't argue with Bardi when it came to bush skills.

'Boss if you find a blackish-grey mud; bring some of that back as well. It's magic mud.

Might have to dig down about two feet under the sand near where you find the plant.'

Bardi watched as John disappeared, suddenly aware of a faint beeping noise coming from behind the tyre he was propped against. He rolled to his good side and felt around under the vehicle. His hand soon retrieved a small black box with a flashing red light. Bardi knew exactly what it was. He turned it over and removed the bottom slide, exposing the battery, which he removed and threw into the bush.

Half an hour later, he heard John coming back. He had the plants and some grey mud in his pannikin. 'Bloody hell Bardi, this shit stinks!'

'Good. That means you got the right stuff. Pass me the plants.'

John watched as Bardi stripped the leaves from the plants, then crushed their roots between two rocks and put it all in a billy can. Pouring in a little water, he asked John to put it on the fire. 'Don't let it boil. Soon as it bubbles, take it off.'

The contents of the billy began to turn a blue colour. When it started to bubble, John lifted it off and put it near Bardi. 'Okay - what now?'

Bardi looked at the grey mud, then stuck his finger into it, testing the consistency of the smelly stuff. 'Okay boss, we're ready. First you gotta take the field dressing off this wound. Once that's off, I can do the rest.'

Feeling somewhat inept, John removed the field dressing, exposing the wound to the elements. Bardi pulled the wound apart, then tipped the hot billy brew straight into the damaged tissue, letting it seep in. Pinching the wound closed with his fingers, his other hand scooped out some of the grey mud, which he smeared over the damage.

'You can put the dressing back on now boss.'

Soon after the operation was complete, Bardi fell into a deep sleep. John checked to see the man had not died on him. To his surprise, Bardi had a very strong pulse rate. The colour in his face began to return. Satisfied, John rose and spread out the papers that Roo had recovered. He looked over the map, and recognised parts of it. It was his old training area. He wondered what the small dots marked on the map represented. Reading through the papers, it seemed likely that the men in the vehicle were trying to escape with the information they had, before being gunned down.

John made himself some tea then took care of the remains of the Air Force Captain. Hanging the man's "dog-tags" onto a makeshift cross which would mark his final resting place for evermore, John said a few words over the grave. On his return, he saw his "patient" resting against the wheel again.

Bardi flicked the small black box over to John. 'We've been tagged.'

John was amazed at how well Bardi looked; bright-eyed and smiling. He stood up as if he had never been wounded and walked a few steps.

'What the hell is this stuff you've treated yourself with?' John demanded incredulously.

'Bush medicine and magic mud.' Bardi laughed as he walked to the fire and took a seat on one of two large rocks.

'Bullshit Bardi! An hour ago you were facing septicaemia. You could hardly move! Now you're up and about like nothing happened.'

'Wait till I remove the dressing. That's going to blow your mind. Two more hours, then we'll get this gauze off and go get your lady.'

John grimaced and shook his head from where he was standing near the Ute. 'Nup. We'll wait till morning Bardi. Roo's due to check in soon.'

'If he's on the other side of those hills' Bardi pointed, 'he's got no chance of his signal getting out. It'll just bounce around in the valley. The magic mud'll stop it getting out but.'

'Magic mud! Bush medicine I can understand, but what gives with this stinking goo?' 'The plant we call Kookoo grass only grows around here. As long as there's Kookoo grass

there's magic mud. My descendant discovered its healing powers years ago. Its medicine is handed to the rightful head fella; the Chief of the tribe. I'm it so I know all about it.' Bardi laughed at John. 'You look like you've seen a ghost Boss.'

'How much does Doc knows about this stuff?'

'He reckons it's a load of mumbo-Garth. Not been tested in a lab. Says he's not going to have anything to do with it.'

'Yeah, that'd be Doc. He's going to join us at Frazer. You can then show the smartarse how well your mumbo Garth works. We better get some shut-eye. Long day tomorrow' John explained, handing Bardi a blanket and pillow.

CHAPTER FIFTEEN

Looking For Jillian

Bardi woke early, prepared breakfast and boiled the billy. Eventually, John eased himself out of his swag, then sat for a moment and lit a smoke, watching his friend walking around as if nothing happened.

'Bardi, what's in that stuff you put on your wound?' he asked, rolling up his "space-blanket" to stow.

'Dunno boss. Somethin' been passed through generations of elders. Like castor oil to you fellas! Bardi grinned cheekily. 'All I know is, it works. Came down from the sky gods.'

'Sky gods! Next you'll be telling me your mob was visited by aliens.'

'True boss. Our tribal elders got heaps from them. Ya reckon that mud is magic? Wait till I show ya what else it can do.'

'Yeah right' said John sceptically, standing up. 'Mud's mud mate. My bet is they'll be cutting your leg off from infection.'

Bardi discarded the field dressing. The skin over the wound had completely repaired itself. Not even a scar was visible. 'Stinking mud ha?' he scoffed, showing the wound site to John.

John's initial astonishment at the curative properties of the mud was heightened as he inspected the site. He had seen many battle wounds. Most that had healed left massive ugly scars. Bardi's was as smooth as the skin around it, and the man was as active as ever. John doubted the intervention of "sky people", but something or someone had passed on the knowledge and Bardi's mob had used it.

He handed John a tin of food. 'You reckon I'm pullin' your leg, eh?'

'Bardi, I was educated in the whitefella way; you were raised out here with your people. Our education comes from life's experiences.'

'You forget Boss – I've seen both sides. I also been to a wadjella school Maybe didn't get degree like you, but this place teach me all I need to know. I've seen both sides, and the grass is not always greener on your side.'

'Point taken Bardi. Are there many of your mob still around these parts?'

'A few. They mostly live on the other side of that ridge. We'll go there now. They'll they tell me if they've seen your woman, and who kidnapped her.'

With Bardi in the lead they set off, closely observing the ground for any tracks left by Jillian's abductors. The men were careful to avoid brushing against clumps of spiky spinifex grass, knowing how quickly its scratches could fester into sores. When an old river-bed came into view, Bardi stopped and watched, only moving forward once he saw a group of kangaroos. John knew it was safe, as the roo's would be nowhere in sight if man was around.

Bardi dug in some white sand, and soon water bubbled into the hole. Taking his pannikin from his webbing he scooped up what John considered to be cold water, given the intense heat that now belted down. Bardi offered him the first drink.

'If the people don't know about this, they're gunna die out here. Sorry Boss; that means the lady as well. Can only last maybe two days without it.'

'Let's hope they're carrying plenty', John replied, thanking Bardi as he handed back the container.

Bardi pointed to some rocks up ahead. 'We go through that gap. The enemy's heading to the big valley; our boys going round the ridge. We can catch 'em if we get 'em in a flank move, but we gotta be quick before they get to the flat rocks. Too hard to track 'em on those.

Bardi found the camp their adversaries had stayed at the previous night, and tested the coals. 'Still warm – they're not far in front of us.'

John nodded. 'How long you think?'

'An hour, maybe two. We'll catch 'em before they get to the rocky flats.'

John's spirit's lifted. He unslung his rifle, pulled the cocking slide back and allowed a round to chamber. Bardi did the same as they headed straight up the slope over the receding spinifex. Small shrubby trees grew from cracks in rocks, holding on to survive.

John was even more on guard due to the snakes he had sighted. Some he recognised as bad; others he had never seen before, like the dark red-skinned variety that seemed to favour rocks. Their skins were almost the same colour as the rocks, giving them ideal camouflage. Unfazed,

Bardi just stepped around them, keeping his eyes peeled for any signs of their quarry's change of direction.

Halfway up the slope, he pointed to a cave. 'Shortcut. We'll be on the other side in half the time.'

The cave was dark, and water could be heard trickling down the rocks. Disturbed, bats flew squawking in the dark. As they inched forward, John flicked his lighter every few steps to check his surrounds. Bardi disappeared up ahead, his skin engulfed by the lack of light in the cave.

Alarmed, John heard what sounded like a faint scuffle. He was relieved when minutes later Bardi returned with two deftly fashioned bush torches.

'Got a light?'

Flicking the lighter, the dry grass and branches exploded in light. Bardi handed John the other torch and touched it on his; the cave's secrets were exposed. As John scanned the light around, he saw a pile of bones. Stunned, he counted at least ten skulls.

'My elders. Their resting place' Bardi explained. He stood near the bones and muttered something in his native lingo. 'I'm asking 'em if we can pass to the chamber.'

'Chamber?' John repeated distractedly, still gazing at the bones. He pondered that this would be the place Bardi would also be laid to rest when he passed on.

'Ya gotta promise me that what you see in the chamber, you'll never mention to anyone.' Bardi sounded very serious.

John promised, though not sure he could keep it. He added, hopefully, 'Give you my word.'

The chamber stood revealed. Light filtered in from an opening overhead and danced over the crystal walls. At the far side, John noticed what he thought was a small pool, but as he walked forward it began to glow. He realised it was not water but a round disk, glowing bright green then pulsating into red and yellow lights.

'Left here by ancestors. Wandjina' Bardi explained, before snapping into combat mode again. 'Come on, we gotta make it to the other side if we want to cut that mob off.'

John was anxious to find Jillian but made a mental note to ask Bardi to take him back to the chamber at some point, as there were items of great interest lying around everywhere. He was still amazed at the round disk pulsing light from itself.

Soundlessly, Bardi continued onward, stooping to pick up an item from one of the ledges. He tucked it into his field jacket and moved towards the passage that would take them to the other side of the ridge.

Roo had followed the side of the ridge, making sure that the leap frog advance was maintained. Cresting a small rise, he lay flat to scan the foreground. Still only spinifex and a small twisted tree. The only thing out of the ordinary was a massive waterfall which roared straight out of some rocks.

He motioned to Adder to have a closer look at some trees in a nearby ravine. Scanning with the heat seeker, Adder made out three shapes. He rechecked to make sure they were not animals, then signalled Roo. He had a hot target. Roo nodded and motioned the others to form a right flank move. The team moved silently into the form-up position. Training had taught them that within two minutes of form-up they would move out towards the target.

Jillian was tied to a tree near a small water hole, stripped of her clothing and shoes. Her body was marked with red welts from the sharp ends of spinifex that had broken off in her skin. Two men in US army uniforms stood over a small fire nearby. The third was at the waterhole trying to catch some fish.

Boomer took the high ground; concealment with a very good field of view. He spoke into his into his lapel mike.

'Three targets. One is sitting at fire, Two is standing, Three at waterhole. No weapons visible near targets. PM tied to tree.'

Roo listened to the report. If there were no weapons visible he wanted to take these men alive. John would be most interested in finding out what the hell was going on.

'Take 'em alive unless weapons appear. Then shoot to wound.'

John stepped out from the cave passage into bright sunlight. Squinting, he allowed his eyes time to adjust. He then had a commanding view of the entire scene below. In shock and rage he took in Jillian's predicament, the small camp and her three captors.

He could also see Roo, positioned to strike. He informed Bardi.

'The shit's about to hit the fan. Skip's in sniper position - looks like they're forming up for a flank attack.'

'Take us half an hour to get to the bottom mate. My bet is you want those blokes alive.' 'Roo'll know that. He'll also know that might put Jillian in danger.'

The American Rangers had no idea that Roo and the boys were so close. Maintaining silence the Rangers were soon placed into the land of nod, with a swift hit from the rifle butts to the back of the head.

Roo soon had them tied and perched against a tree.

John and Bardi made haste getting down the ridge. Once on flat ground they ran towards the bush patch. Fletch and Dicko were the first to swing around, weapons levelled. If not for Adder's warning yell, both men would be lying dead.

Roo smiled, then looked at Bardi, 'What the fuck? You were shot in the hip man! Now you're running around like a jackrabbit.'

'Bush magic Roo, we blackfellas know lots of magic.' Bardi grinned at John.

Jillian was cut down and John wrapped and zipped his field coat around her naked body.

The men had the three American's tied up. Giving his captives a death stare, Dicko picked up Jillian's clothes from the ground, and handed them back to her. Electrical ties bound the prisoners' hands behind them. Dicko was not fussed about how tight he pulled the black plastic strips. He could see them cutting into the flesh. He pushed Jillian's attackers down onto the ground and kicked them, making sure they moved back to where he wanted them. He then knelt down, resting on his rifle.

'Now you ranger fellas are pretty smart. The Boss is coming over to have a chat with you. My advice is - talk, or we give you to that blackfella there,' he warned, pointing at Bardi. 'Around here is his country. Lots of his tribe in these parts. Roasted American is a delicacy here.'

As if on cue, Bardi ran toward the men, snarling like a wild beast. He snapped his gums open and closed, showing his teeth, then performing a tribal dance in front of them.

'He is picking out which one of you is going to be first on the dinner plate' Dicko said, just as a group of six more Aboriginals walked into the camp. They carried spears and wore only lap- laps around their waists. Dicko laughed, thinking it could not have been planned better.

One went over to Bardi, and greeted him in his tribal fashion, of a hand shake back slapping and then lowering his head to indicate to Bardi he was subordinate to him.

Bardi then walked toward the other five, who all bowed their heads as he spoke to them, acknowledging him as the elder of what remained of their tribe. They showed utter respect for the man.

'You pick 'em tucker from that mob' Bardi said, not showing any emotion. The six men walked over to the three rangers and began to feel them all over.

'Them all too skinny except this fella, maybe get a feed from him,' one of the bush Aboriginals said to Bardi.

'Okay, take him away.'

The six men cut the electrical tie, stood the man up and dragged him off into the bushes.

Soon a blood-curdling scream coming from that direction.

'Him tucker now' Bardi said to Dicko.

The looks on the faces of the other two Americans showed complete horror, as if they believed yet did not want to believe what had happened.

One of the Aboriginals returned with a lump of bloodied meat slung over his shoulder. He dumped it down in front of the other two.

'You got any special request for meat cuts?' the black fella asked placing the lump of meat directly onto the fire. It was not possible to tell if it was man or animal. The two Americans looked at each other; one turned away and spewed his guts up. The five other Aboriginals returned covered in roo blood. They sat down ensuring the American soldiers could see their blood stained bodies, and yammered away in their own tongue.

John Kelly came over and cut the tie on one of the captives. 'You ready for a chat or do I give you to the blacks?'

The man looked at the meat cooking on the fire, then at his friend still tied up. 'What do you want to know?'

John checked behind his ear, three dots.

'Okay, fella from the top, or chop-chop like him.' He pointed to the fire.

As the American got up he turned to his buddy.

'I heard the blacks over here were cannibals, but didn't figure they still did this. My God! What do I tell the Sergeants wife and kids? Daddy eaten by humans?'

Stricken, he stared at the meat on the fire.

'Sorry man. I never thought it would come to this.'

The Aboriginals were now chanting, jumping and stamping in front of the fire, poking at the meat as it sizzled on the coals.

Roo and John escorted the distressed man away. John called Jillian over to join them. The American revealed what he said he knew, although John had his doubts. Some of it he knew to be true; the parts about Devils Rock and the President who took over.

The man was in tears by the time he finished. John re-tied his wrists and returned him to his buddy, then turned to Roo and Jillian.

'What do you think?'

'Got a few things right. May be something in what he told us. He's shit-scared that his buddy's being cooked on that fire. Obviously doesn't want to end up the same way.'

Roo laughed. 'Should have seen the looks on their faces when that blackfella carried in the lump of meat! Shit, never got a camera when you really need one.'

Jillian looked at John. 'If what he said is true, then Australia is really treated like another state of the US, but with uncontrollable threats that we as a nation can't fight with our limited military forces. God Dad! You've really sold us out.'

CHAPTER SIXTEEN

Frazer's Homestead

By the time the vehicles rolled to a stop in front of the dilapidated building which was once the stately home of the pioneering Frazer family, it was getting dark.

John soon had the portable generators fired up, with the aid of two flood lamps. Light danced over the remains of the house. It was not long before Roo gave the bad news to his fading fighters. He wants two on patrol all night.

'Asp you get the patrol organised. Two hours on Four off. That everyone is to take a turn.' Roo gave his orders.

Bardi had a meal on the small fire he had built. Dicko had made a bush shower for Jillian, shading it off with a role of hessian he had found in the rear of one of the utes.

John sat with Bardi as he tended to the meal. 'How long do you think those three will last?'

'Maybe two days - if the snakes don't get them first. The spinifex'll poison their blood, given they've got no shoes or clothing. Not much water around either, the way they'll have to go to get back to their camp.'

John laughed. 'So Bardi, how did you contact your men to tell them what to do?' 'Blackfella magic boss. I've said it once and I'll say it again - we know a lot about our country.' Bardi patted gently on the mirror he had placed in his jacket pocket in the cave.

John then outlined their American prisoner's confession to his trusted friend, asking 'You know any faster way to Indigo? Where we won't be detected?'

Bardi thought for a while. 'Maybe. The spirits of the elders would want me to defend this country. I've got an idea but it will be tough going for all. Not sure if she will make it.' He pointed to the makeshift shower.

'Jillian's got spunk mate - she hasn't complained thus far.'

'She can't go the way we gotta go. Secret place. Men only' Bardi insisted. 'What about the Elders? Can't they give permission?'

Bardi scraped at his small goatee beard. 'Maybe. Have to see when I ask them.' 'When?'

'Tonight. I'll go to a special place and ask 'em. Now you tell them all dinner is ready.'

Next morning, Jillian and John were the last out of bed. Roo had woken the men early, and was putting them through a gruelling cardio-vascular battle workout.

As the troop went through its paces, John remembered when he had selected each member to train for his special squad - Strike Team Delta. The higher command of the army had dismissed it as a waste of time. However, the politicians found a way to use his elite team for their own dubious ambitions – to the detriment of the nation. Ignorant of their leaders' double agenda, the crack company never complained about the operations they were called on to perform, often in hazardous and harsh conditions.

John was brought back to reality by the arresting sight of Jillian exiting the house dressed in jeans and one of his sweat shirts. He noticed her small tits jumping around in his shirt, and the outline of her buttocks as she walked a sight sexy enough to make any man look twice.

Roo still had the men running, his voice breaking the quiet of the early morning. 'What are they doing?' Jillian asked, sitting down near John.

'Getting fit love. I told them last night what we are up against. They all want to help get this nation back on its feet with a real government in power.'

He looked over at her. 'No offence meant to you.'

'None taken. After everything that's happened, I find it hard to believe that you guys are still keen to help.'

'You can dislike your enemy, that's healthy, but never turn on your country. Most of all, never turn on your friends, no matter what.'

'Well said darling' Jillian murmured approvingly.

'My father's words. He was a soldier too. Special Forces, like me. An SAS commander in the Korean War.'

'Yes, I remember you saying now. Soldiering runs in the family.' 'Yep. The old man was the founding father of Strike Force Delta.' 'All the way back to Ned Kelly as I recall?'

'That's a stretch, though mum's great-great grandfather was involved in the Eureka Stockade. So I guess our blood line has been rebellious all the way through.'

'I reckon old Ned was trying to do the right thing. Bit of a Robin Hood type.' Jillian said. 'Nuh. He was a killer and a bully. I don't condone what he did.' John lit a smoke and drew

back on it. 'So - what do you think about your old man now?' This was a question Jillian would have preferred to avoid.

'For the good of the nation, he has to be stopped. He's a traitor. People trusted him, voted him in, and he's used his Prime Ministership for his own gains. That is not what politics is about.'

John laughed a little. 'In a way all politics is the same.' 'What do you mean?'

'Well look at it. When you become a member or leader of a party, you don't have your own conscience vote. You toe the party line or you're out. At least Independents can vote for what people elect them to do.

Parties don't listen to the people. They have "behind the scenes" people dictating what they think is the best way forward, for the party, not the people. Is that fair?' John drew on his smoke again.

'For example - what they did to me and my men. Not good for the people. It hides a lot of lies. The party has to cover it up or lose the next election. The new government's bound to find out what happened. That's what scares your people most of all, but who suffers? The people who elected the cheats and liars.'

'Do you put me in that basket?' Jillian asked.

'If the cap fits! You're a party person. Do you do everything that is voted on behind closed doors? You know - the "secrets" room?

'Doesn't what I am doing now show you I care?'

'You were coerced Jillian. You know that if we uncover the truth, your party are unlikely to rule this country again.'

'It may be to our benefit! Honesty and all that.'

'I take it you're planning to stay in politics then? No Utopia for you?' 'I feel a responsibility to the people.'

'No, to the party. If you believed in the people you'd be opening this country up. Running our power on solar and wind. Pumping sea water from the north to make fresh water for the outback, and granting the land there to people who can make a go of it. But no, the universal political flaw prevails. Preserving party power, even if it means compromising ideals. Carrot- dangling at election time's as far as it goes.'

'I love your passion John.'

'See those men there?' He pointed.

'Yep.'

'Who's going to reward them for all they've done and are about to do? Your party? Are they really going to get their lives back? Wives and families? Stolen assets? Yet they don't hesitate to take on this mission, knowing they could die. Why? Because they promised one thing: to serve their people with pride and honour. The enlistment oath they took never expires. That conviction is needed if this nation is to become truly great. Sadly lacking in short-sighted, self-interested people and parties.'

'John, how come you let those Americans go yesterday?'

'The elements will take care of them. If they make it back to their own kind it'll be in our favour. They'll know we're onto them.'

'If? Don't you mean when?'

'Bardi gives them two or three days at best out bush.' 'So where does this leave us?' Jillian asked.

John looked over at Jillian, the mother of his son, and saw only her beauty. 'When this is all over it'll be time to wipe the slate clean and start over.

'Utopia?' Jillian asked with a wry smile.

'Why not? Why not hundreds of Utopias? Thousands! Run by people weary of political clap- trap. You can help make it happen.'

CHAPTER SEVENTEEN

Frazer's. Bardi returns.

Bardi wandered back to the homestead and put down his dilly bag. Taking a glass of water, he sat down with John and Jillian.

'I reckon I got permission - from the spirits of the Elders. But you gotta take some our mob along to keep an eye on things.'

'I think we can agree to that, but your people will have to get some training from Roo' John replied.

'Good.'

Bardi stood up and whistled. From the shelter of the scrub came six Aboriginal men, the ones who had helped out at the water hole.

'My trusty warrior mates knew you couldn't say no.' He gave the widest grin.

'Any tucker left?'

Adder was now sitting under the shade of a large tree, a pile of fifty cal ammo on the ground in front of him. He then began to pull the head out of each cartridge and top it up to its former filling point.

The rest of their small camp was similarly busy. Men serviced vehicles, cleaned weapons and completed all other tasks necessary to their impending mission.

Overseeing the activities, Roo paced around the groups, ensuring the men had not lost their training in these vital tasks.

John, Bardi and his six man tribe were discussing the best plan of attack. It was imperative they got it right. None knew what they were up against.

Dicko had rigged up a makeshift satellite dish. He had a compass and was trying to figure out the location needed for it to pick up a signal. Any satellite would do.

His computer attached, he began to tune, entering keyboard instructions for the computer to accept signals from satellites within range of the improvised dish. He got a lock. Triumph, Dicko marked the point on the dish and ground, then sat down to surf the internet? on the WWW.

Dicko yelled for John. 'Hey Boss! Want the latest news?' he yelled excitedly.

John, Jillian and some of the others came running over as Dicko pulled up the latest Sky news report. It was hammering a sensational story. The Prime Minister had deserted her post and the political situation was in chaos. People being interviewed gave their version of events, ranging from abduction by aliens to kidnap and murder by terrorists. The bottom line was she had lost her position and a new politician elevated to the position of PM. Jillian listened for the name of her successor. It was Garry Grey.

'My God John, he's so far up my father's arse he has to stick his head out of his ear to breathe! We're back to square one.'

'Have you still got trusted friends in Canberra? I mean, people who will do exactly as you ask, perhaps even kill for you if need be?'

'I think so, but obviously not within the public service.' 'How about the military?'

'Yes, a few of the Generals and unit commanders would stand by me, although they'll be under the impression I am missing, presumed dead, as per that radio broadcast.

'Maybe. Maybe not. We need to get a message to the one you trust the most.' 'That'd be General Colin Heart. He's Chief of Operations, Army.'

'Yes, I know Colin. A good man and a good soldier. If our Air Force Captain was telling the truth, then I figure the Defence Secretary knows a bit. The Def Sec is ranked below General Heart, so we might be half-way there. Just got to get a message to him - and it must be secure.

'Could email him Boss,' Dicko replied.

'Ha! He wouldn't even know how to turn a computer on -his staff officer'd do all that.' Jillian smiled.

'Snail mail then. I know his home address. We need to find a post office.'

'The mail truck comes to the community on Wednesdays' offered Bardi. 'Drops it off, picks it up.'

John smiled.

'You never cease to amaze me Bardi. Got an answer for everything.' 'Bush magic Boss.'

Bardi winked.

John leaned over to Dicko.

'See if you can work your computer magic to find out about the New World Command, and what they're up to. Also if the Yanks are still backing the Australian government.'

Dicko nodded.

'Just gotta get a hot feed into a US government computer system.' He took a CD from his computer bag and looked at it.

'Hope you still work baby.'

Inserting the disk, he pressed "Enter." The silver disk had retrieved a lot of information over the years. Dicko had written its code-breaking program while studying computer science, using systems that were high-tech then. His only concern was "How sophisticated are computer codes now?"

'Soon find out' he thought, immersing himself into the murky recesses of technology.

Garry Grey faced the remaining members of his political party, and spoke in reassuring tones.

'Look, we still have the numbers; we don't need to make radical changes to our aims at the moment. The opposition has no idea what's going on. As far as they're concerned the PM has jumped ship. We keep tight lipped about her and soldier on.'

'What if she has in fact been kidnapped? Is there any truth in the rumour about this mystery bloke John Kelly resurfacing?' one of the ministers asked.

'Kelly is yesterday's news. Procedures have been put in place to make it impossible for him or his offsiders to resurface. We have to remain focused and united in this. Back away and we tumble.'

'So you'll wave a magic wand and it'll all go away?' Came a mocking question from the far end of the table.

'No, but our American friends will take care of it. They'll have to if they want to retain Indigo.'

Someone at the table muttered, just loud enough that others could hear,

'Some of us predicted this'd happen if we got involved with the Yanks. We're no better than they are. We'll be just as guilty as them if this goes on.'

'You got something to say, Mister Brown?' challenged Grey, revelling in his newfound power.

'Just this. As of now, I don't want anything to do with this bizarre plan of yours. You're all fucking mad.'

Brown stood up.

'Last chance people, if you wish to walk away.' No-one stood.

'Be it on your heads then.'

He walked from the room, feeling free for the first time in his life. From now on he would say and do as he pleased.

Frazer's Homestead

A few of the team members came over to John. 'Boss, we were promised our ID's, plus back pay and all that other shit when we got here. So far - nothing.'

'Beginning to wonder about that myself,' said John apologetically, raising his eyebrows as he looked at his men. 'I'll have a word to the PM.'

Jillian was sitting at the dilapidated kitchen table inside the building. She saw John come in. 'Trouble?' she asked.

'Could say that. The men want to know when you're going to deliver on the promise; you know, ID's and such.'

'It'll get here John. These things take time. After all, we've only been here one day.'

'I accept that, but don't think the men are going to swallow it.' Jillian's tone changed. John had never heard her talk like she did.

'Well they're your soldiers. You'll have to pull them into line if this is going to be resolved in the positive. Given what we've seen on those news flashes, they may have to wait till I'm back in the PM's chair.'

'That'll never happen and you know it!' John barked back at her. 'If you think that's what it'll take I'll arrange for your transport back to Canberra right now.'

'You know that would cost me my life. Is that what you want?'

'No, we want what was promised to us. Nothing more, nothing less. If you won't act, I'll get Dicko onto the bloke who took over your spot to start the ball rolling. He's got a week to deliver.'

'Otherwise?'

'We join Bardi and his tribe and start kicking Canberra's arse from out here. Our story will be told Jillian.' John stormed from the room.

Jillian sat thinking of what had just happened. She knew there was no way the power players in Canberra would concede. As far as they were concerned, John and his Delta team were dead. She then wondered about Dale - had he planned her downfall for his own gain?

Jillian was getting very lonely about now. Her colleagues in Canberra were jumping like rats from a sinking ship. Would they be loyal upon her return? She feared not.

Roo was resting. John wandered over and offered his best operative a cold beer.

'Everything ready?'

'Close. Where in the hell did you get these?' Roo pointed to the cold beers. 'Back of the ute. There's two cans for each man tonight.'

Roo stood up, walked over to the tree and had a piss. 'What is it we really have to do?'

'Stop whatever is going on at Indigo and no, I'm not really sure of the true story.'

'Are we doing this for your girlfriend or for our country? The men are pissed off with not having their papers and pay. Boss, just be damn sure this isn't another set up like Devils.' Roo finished peeing and turned back to John.

'Frankly, I don't know who to trust anymore.'

'You think we should walk away from this?' John asked.

'Dunno Boss; bit of a rock and a hard place. Just don't know who's pulling the strings. We'll stick with your call.'

CHAPTER EIGHTEEN

Gulls Flat, Range View Farm

Dale remained sitting on the spare bed of the guest house. He had all the files that John had left spread out on the floor. He was reading them when Sandra walked in with two cups of coffee. She bought a chair in from the kitchen and sat down, passing a cup to Dale. She sipped from hers.

'Find anything?'

Dale put the file down and sipped his coffee.

'Yep, and I don't like what I'm seeing. Reckon Mrs. Gillman would let me look at the other files David has stashed over yonder?'

'I think if you explain it properly she'll agree. She has nothing to hide and no real idea what her husband is up to. I think your biggest problem will be getting John to trust you.'

'Yeah, he'd be a very mixed up, suspicious fella right now, and why not? I need to get back to Canberra and do some more soul searching. I'm sure the real answer is there. It's just a matter of finding it.'

Washington, USA

1621 Fifth Avenue was not much different to the many other buildings along the street. Entering the building was like stepping back in time. In one corner was an old book shop; alongside that was a take-away burger joint, then a news stand. A stately staircase ascended its way to the second floor, with a security guard posted at the bottom to prevent any unwanted eyes getting a peek at the floor above.

David Gillman walked to the security guard, showed his ID and began to climb the stairs. A laser-controlled moment sensor system cut in, scanning his body to match against records stored in the computer system. Failure to match meant an intruder would be gassed on reaching the first landing, the body quickly disposed of through a false floor to the basement below, then turned into garden fertiliser and sold to the public at a store not far from 1621.

As David made it to the security door on Level One he was signed in and given a disk to put on his jacket. The disk would continually be scanned to monitor his every move within the building. His disk colour was Indigo (deep blue.) This gave him access to the most secure areas of the building, including the large conference room, whose walls were adorned with very impressive paintings of the Masters of the New World Council. The current Masters were now in conference around an expansive oval meeting table. They sat in large leather chairs, each fitted with a swing arm that held a small screen and headphones.

In attendance were the US Secretary of Defence, a representative from the royal family and six of the world's wealthiest men. At the end of the oval table sat an Arab named Nadir who was the Master General.

Nadir was an oil billionaire who preferred western culture to his own. He set the world's oil prices, levering them up or down depending on his mood each morning. Nadir was no longer happy with his twenty percent ownership. He wanted all the oil reserves still in the ground in the Middle East. This monopoly would promote him to Grand Master of the entire Middle East, controlling everything moving in or out of its many ports.

Sitting at Nadir's right hand was the President of the United States, Darren Philips, a Texan whose wealth came also from oil. His aim was to control the Americas, Australia and the greater parts of Asia, whose wealth and commodities would be needed for the New World.

Suddenly, the agitated face of the NWC's youthful Information and Technology officer appeared at the door. He made a beeline for the Secretary of Defence and whispered into his ear.

Nadir noticed, and banged a small wooden hammer on the table. 'If you please - address the entire meeting.'

The IT officer looked at the Master General, then stood and straightened his tie. When he tried to address the assembly, his voice cracked with apprehension, and no words would come out.

'Generals,' he began, then took a sip of water. 'Our system security has been breached.'

Silence fell over the meeting. Members glanced around at each other, looking for someone to blame.

Nadir swung around in his chair, pen in hand. He tapped it against his palm, then leant forward.

'How far in?'

'Indigo sir,' the IT officer replied.

'Well that is not too bad is it? Indigo only shows statistics of world numbers and future food needs. It poses little problem.'

'Sir, they've hacked into our operational files, the whole nine yards. Copies have been downloaded.'

Nadir stood up, his face red, and glared at his employee.

'You assured me the encrypted files would never be breached. Now you stand here telling us our most classified project to date has been breached. Well tell me, my technical genius, who has this information now?'

'I don't know sir. I've narrowed it down to someone in Australia. That's as close as I can get.'

All eyes fell on David Gillman; he looked uncomfortable in his chair. A recent phone-call from his wife had divulged Jillian's news of John Kelly's return. He stood up.

'Master General, I believe I know who has done this.' Nadir was terse.

'Who?'

'John Kelly' he admitted reluctantly, knowing he had most likely signed his own death warrant.

'He was taken care of after the mishap on Devils Rock. Collateral damage. How can a dead man be doing this?' Nadir enquired in a chilling undertone.

'I couldn't give the order to have him killed. He is my grandson's father.' Stonily, the Master General replied,

'You have failed to abide by our ruling. You understand the consequence.'

David nodded, his mind racing. He now faced a lethal injection. The NWC's doctors would issue the death certificate: Cardiac Arrest. His body would be cremated.

Nadir took the floor again.

'We will finish this mission as it was first planned. Our operatives will track down and dispatch John Kelly. Objections?'

With a look of subtle but unmistakeable triumph, the Secretary of Defence winked at the President. Total control of Australia would now be theirs.

No one spoke against the counter-attack. The meeting ended abruptly and the Generals began to leave. Some passed David and shook his hand with an air of finality.

Outside, the Defence Secretary sat at the coffee shop with the President. He smiled.

'We'll have General Taylor commence operation "Wipeout" as soon as Indigo is done with.' 'Now that's a plan. I'll have the delivery bought forward. We have six flights going to Indigo this week. The hardware will fit on all.'

The Secretary of Defence grinned, imagining the wealth he would soon command.

CHAPTER NINETEEN

Frazer's Homestead, Australia

Dicko bought his findings from the search to John. Quietly, he stood looking down at the folder of papers he had just presented.

'I think you had better study those print-outs. If I understand what they're saying, this country has a real problem.'

John looked at the papers; one thing he liked to have was Intelligence before any mission that might put his team in harm's way.

'Have Roo come over. He'll need to look these over as well. No, muster the whole team, Bardi's mob as well.

Dicko turned and walked off to where Roo was helping with the last of the fifty cal bullets.

Indigo Base Camp

Dressed in his field fatigues, General Mike Taylor emerged from his five star residences, smoking a large cigar. He appraised the hundreds of Indigo workers who had each paid ten thousand dollars to ensure they would not be victims of the Master Plan.

He looked out over the land. Outback Australia was unlike any country he had ever served in during his many years in the American military. Like the prairies of his homeland the terrain was undulating, with many ridges. Nearby was thick forest, watered by the catchment from large limestone ridges that encircled the entire area. He felt safe at the base; no satellites could get an image of his hideaway. The workers could be on the job 24/7 when needed.

Construction of the silos had exceeded expectation in the ten months since they began, and would soon be ready for their intended purpose. A recent classified dispatch had informed him that another seven sites would be needed. "Wipeout" was now part of a plan he had originally co-conceived.

Master Sergeant Barry Pillman looked up as Taylor approached.

'We got a little problem needs taking care of. Our old nemesis John Kelly is back on the scene. You remember Kelly from Devils?'

'I do Sir. This time he won't walk away. I have just the team to take care of this splinter in our foot.'

Pillman remembered Kelly; he was the team leader who was eventually blamed for the President's chopper crash. Pillman had set the wheels in motion that would lead to Kelly's downfall. It was a simple plan. The current President who was at the time of Devils wanted talks the Vic President did not wish to have talks with Bin Ladin. When the plan to bring down the President chopper was made, Kelly and his strike team would be made to take the fall. He had set Kelly up with the duplicate Red Eye missile complete with matching serial numbers. A small force of Americans would take out the Presidents chopper, capture Kelly and his Strike team and lay blame on the downing of the chopper.

Evidence would be the fired Red Eye that had the same serial number that was issued to Kelly for protection against air strikes in his sector. As General Taylor was the UN base commander on Devils and also high up in the NWC would present the fact at Kelly's Court Martial. The Vice President would take office, being a high ranking NWC member meant that Project Indigo and more to the point "Wipeout." Was all go. The grand plan to take control of the world, reduce the population to a sustainable amount. NWC would control the world food, oil and other commodities. The citizens of the world would pay top price just to stay alive.

Pillman remembered that Kelly would be killed under the act of War. He didn't realise that as a coalition force Kelly would be given back to his own country for disciplinary action. But General Taylor assured all that Kelly would not live to try and stop the NWC in achieving its objective. Devils Rock was British and still under their rule. As Indigo was discovered to have the same properties as Devils Rock and was available, the deal was struck.

Neither Taylor nor Pillman figured Kelly would re-appear. He was dangerous and knew too much to be considered just a splinter. If he was alive that meant his entire Strike Team was still very much in the land of the living. He had to be taken care of, the American way.

Believing Kelly had been taken out of the equation NWC was given Indigo to build the launch sites in secret, they would continue to fund the government to re-gain the chair of power over and over again.

Frazer's Station

Jillian came over to where the men had gathered. John stopped talking when she came into earshot.

'No need to stop on my account.' She smiled at the group of men.

John put down the files. 'Sorry - this is operational stuff.' 'I thought I was part of this too?'

'Not operations. Sorry.' John said.

Vanquished, Jillian turned and walked back toward the remains of the homestead. Going inside, she noticed where Dicko had now placed the computer with a lead to the satellite dish. She looked at the cable end, then at the jack lead she had for her mobile phone connection to a car antenna.

She checked the end; it fitted to the computer, but would there be reception? When Jillian plugged it into her phone, two small bars appeared. She quickly sent a text message, then removed the cable and put it back in her jeans pocket along with the mobile phone.

Bardi came in just in time to see Jillian reinsert the dish cable into the computer.

'What're you doing with that?' he asked.

Jillian jumped with fright.

'Nothing! I saw it hanging down and wondered what it was. It's a cable I think.'

'Yes it is, one that connects us to the outside. You know that.' He walked over to where she was standing.

'Hand it over.' 'What?'

'The mobile phone and jump-lead you put in your pocket. I saw you from the door.' Bardi held his hand out.

'I was just seeing if I could get a signal. I wanted to ring mum.' 'Bullshit. Give it to me' Bardi insisted.

She handed them over.

'Figure you're going to tell John now?'

'I keep no secrets from my boss,' he replied.

'Keep this one a secret and I'll make it worth your while' Jillian said lightly.   'You couldn't pay me enough. So – I reckon you might've been in on our going missing after Devils? You, your political party and your old man.'

'I didn't know anything until I became Prime Minister. That's the truth.'

'You let the father of your child disappear into the never-never so your party could remain in power. The only thing that comes out of your mouth is bullshit.'

Bardi reached out and pulled her hair aside. No dot was seen. He released her. 'Why?'

'For fuck's sake! I was organising for your money and ID's to be sent. Go on, check my last message.'

John, who was standing outside, had overheard the entire conversation. He felt his guts being ripped out. A big question remained. Why had they been kept alive? Walking away from the door, he took out a beer, sat down and pulled off the rip-top. He squeezed the can as he drained it of its contents, then took another and did the same. Roo was in the bush shower. John went over and stood near the hessian wall.

'Stop the training mate. We're not doing this mission.'

Roo had soap all over his face. He spat some out, ducked under the shower head and pulled down on the rope. Water trickled over his bald head, flushing the soap away.

'So the promise is a no go?'

'It appears we have been exposed. The NWC can now have a fair old crack at us. Indigo is all bullshit.'

'Dicko's readouts don't say that. For God's sake Boss, they're going to launch half a dozen chemical missiles from our soil into the Middle East in the name of the New World. Thousands of innocent people are going to die.'

'Roo, they didn't give a shit about us after Devils. We had to live like tip dogs for near on twenty years, looking over our shoulders day and night. For what? For nothing.'

It was pretty dam smart of the government to get themselves into a bind, then get Dale to set us to get them out. Owe the big promise of our freedom back. Not to mention the back-pay and all our assets returned. Shit Roo, why didn't I see this coming?'

All they're using us for is to give NWC more power We find a weakness in their security and they tighten it. Their outfit is impenetrable. They will win this battle.'

Roo let the rope go and stepped out of the shower buck naked to face John. 'You gutless bastard. I've never known you to be a quitter!'

He swung his right fist, hitting John hard in the face. With a retaliatory swing, John landed two powerful hits on Roo, who shook his head.

'Haven't lost your touch.' Roo said

He then ran at John, bear-hugged him and threw him to the ground. He held John's head in a vice-like grip and spoke point-blank into his ear.

'If there's a sniff of hope of ever getting my ID back, then I'm going for it.'

Roo slowly released his grip then stood up. John eased himself to his knees, scowling at Roo. 'Ever the optimist.'

'No. It's our code. Never give in. We are one, brother. Remember that Boss? You drummed it into us.'

John smiled up at Roo in gratitude, then took his outstretched hand and was pulled to his feet. 'You of all people Boss. You're not a quitter. Never have been. Wouldn't that be a team decision?' Roo asked, throwing a towel at John.

'Why do you think those men came out of hiding to help us? Because we're on our way to reclaim our lives, as brothers. Are you fanny-struck now? Wrapped around her little finger?'

'Ask the men, then get back to me.'

John walked off, rubbing his jaw ruefully. He had a loose tooth. His heart wanted to trust Jillian but his thoughts rebelled. He washed and cleaned his face, noticing bruising around one eye. Suddenly, Bardi's men emerged from the bush, carrying a large canvas Australia Post bag.

'That chopper driver; remember 'im? Postie delivered this to the community for your Boss' one of them said, placing the bag on the ground near Bardi.

Adder, Dicko and Fletch came over. 'What ya got there Bardi?' Fletch asked, pointing to the bag.

'Delivery for the Boss.'

Bardie took control of the bag, fearing his comrades might beat him to it. 'You mob seen him lately?'

'Ya he over at the water tank licking his wounds.'

Adder pointed in the direction of the tank they had repaired to hold fresh water. Bardi nodded, picked up the bag and walked to where John was still tending his wounds.

'Roo give you a bit of a touch up?'

'Yep. Forgot how hard the bastard can hit. What've you got there?' 'Mail for ya, from the Community. Special delivery.'

John finished cleaning himself up, then picked up the bag and walked towards the house. Passing the makeshift shower that had been put up for Jillian, he saw her naked outline behind the curtain. His heart skipped a little. He wanted so much to jump in the shower and join her but held back, rattled.

John resolutely walked away. He put the mailbag on the table and unclipped its lock, tipping out the contents. There were eleven shoe-box sized packages, each addressed to a Delta strike team member. Each man's correct original rank prefaced the names on the packages.

John opened his. Birth certificate. Tax file number. The titles to his house in Perth, and a bank passbook, debit card and four digit pin number. A statement slip read "Damages Settlement: Ten million and five hundred thousand dollars.

John closed the bank book and sat down, trying to take in what he had just seen. A sheet of notepaper at the bottom of the box read "As promised. Good luck." On the reverse was an update on Indigo. Scanning it, John's hair prickled the back of his neck. It was a feeling he often got before going on a major operation. He ran to the door.

'Muster parade in ten!' He yelled to Roo, the man who had reminded him who he was.

CHAPTER TWENTY

Indigo Base Camp

Master Sergeant Barry Pillman finished inspecting his guardsmen, then stepped inside and spoke to the commander.

'All operational?'

'All good, Sergeant. We've installed the movement sensors. They extend 200 yards from the main fence. Anyone who tries to cross will be picked up. We're waiting on the automatic machine-gun posts, but they should be up and running tomorrow.'

'Good. Carry out regular patrols and tower duty till they come on line.'

Pillman looked over at a dozen soldiers resting on their beds. He nodded, walked out to his jeep then drove off toward the large building near the end of the fence. It contained most of the supplies for the camp, including weapons.

The Sergeant was challenged by a guard at the door, then allowed to enter. Inside was a high ceiling with down-lights casting a ghostly glow onto the floor. Boxes of weapons and ammunition were stacked at one side. Near them, a row of larger boxes read "MISSILE."

Five large rockets were concealed under tarpaulins. He walked over and tapped one of them. 'Soon my little friends you will be flying.'

A store worker came over. 'You the security head bloke?'

'Yes. Master-Sergeant Pillman. What can I do for you?' He introduced himself. 'Was told to give you these. They came in on a flight this morning.'

He handed him the Manifesto from the aircraft.

Pillman looked over the papers, seven short range missiles and 500 litres of 72-hour active nerve gas. He thanked the storeman then tucked the papers into his pocket and walked off the way he had come.

He stopped at General Taylor's bunk-house and knocked on the door. Several minutes passed. Suddenly the door opened and a girl in her underwear dashed past him and ran down the road, carrying her clothes.

'Sergeant, this little visit had better be bloody worth it,' Taylor said, looking past him as the girl was slowly engulfed in the fading light.

Pillman handed over the manifesto.

'I think this will justify the disruption.'

Viewing it, the General invited Pillman in. They sat in a lounge room in leather chairs. 'Drink, Sergeant?' Taylor asked, preparing two glasses of whiskey. He handed one to the Sergeant, took his own and sat down.

'Do you realise what this manifesto means?'

Pillman leaned forward in his chair; he looked long at the General.

'Got a bit of an idea. More cities?'

'Well ... yes. How'd you like to be a co-owner of this continent, with all its wealth?' 'The Gold Nugget of the world, Sir? A dream come true - as long as you're the General

Master.'

'I can assure you, I'm not going anyplace Sergeant.'

Taylor smiled, then explained that the short range missiles were going to make it happen.

'We now need to concentrate on getting the launch systems up and running. My understanding is that our Commander in the States will be sending the exact computer codes and targeting info soon. You are to get your best IT man onto it.'

He looked at his wrist watch.

'We got six weeks from today, May 1. June 16 is D-Day.' Pillman nodded.

'That's a realistic time frame. But what about this Kelly fella? There's been no further information on him or what he's up to.'

'We find him and eliminate him.'

Frazer's Station; Homestead

Delta Team was abuzz with their newfound liberty: town, the ability to stroll into a bank, or simply buy a beer and even a car if they wanted to. The parcels had provided their freedom. Roo made sure they all showered and shaved. He was just as excited. Bardi had gone back to his community to collect the 20-seater bus that would take them to Alice Springs.

'Hey John, is she coming?' Roo said, pulling on clean jeans and tucking in his shirt. 'I guess so. Give me a chance to check a few things out.'

'Find out who sent the packages?' Roo raised an eyebrow.

'No, not yet,' John replied, hoping it was Jillian but too afraid to believe it. '$200 it was her office,' Roo said, combing his hair.

The bus arrived. Bardi was at the wheel. He opened the automatic doors. 'Non-stop bus to Alice. All aboard.'

They filed in and sat down. John and Jillian took a seat at the rear. The doors closed and soon it was moving, a two hour trip to Alice ahead of them.

Jillian turned to John.

'What's the first thing you're going to do?'

'Go to the bank, draw out some of my own money, get pissed without worrying who's looking at me, then book a motel room and sleep it off.'

'Am I in on any of that?' she asked, putting her hand into his. 'Maybe, if you come clean with me.'

'About what?' Jillian asked.

John took her hand and squeezed it a little.

'The packages.'

'The packages. Yes, well - I organised them via Dale a while back obviously. When Bardi came in and found me on the computer, I was messaging Dale to tell him where we were, that's all. You overheard the whole thing, I know. Do you think I'm mixed up with this NWC?'

'It crossed my mind. Too many things have happened for me to think otherwise.'

'Even though you now have your birth certificates, compensation money, tax files numbers and title deeds to your properties?'

'Well... top scores on that. So, you better show me how to use this bankcard thingy. Never had 'em in my day.' John laughed.

Alice Springs

It was 2pm when the bus pulled into Alice Springs. There were lots of tourists in town. John noticed registration plates from nearly every state in Australia. Along with the rest of his men, their first port of call was the bank. He looked at the ATM and was still stumped. Jillian appeared and took his card.

'How much do you want?' she asked, her fingers hovering over the keypad.

'Couple of grand should do,' John replied. The thought he was actually getting his own money bought a smile to his face.

'I'll try, but you may have a limit of a thousand per day.'

Jillian punched in the correct numbers and voila! Two thousand dollars in fifties was delivered.

'Amazing! Plastic pulchritude! The Martians have landed!' John said with a very large grin. 'Only if you have money in the bank for starters,' Jillian laughed. She stayed at the teller machine and, one at a time, showed each team member how to use it.

Dicko asked 'Can I use this to buy stuff in shops?'

'Yep. Just give 'em the card. They'll ask what type of account, then you put in your secret PIN number. It pays for the goods and you get your card back' Jillian explained.

Dicko took his cash, and then walked off.

'Going shopping,' he said, and headed for a shop he had seen from the bus on the way in. It sold computers and satellite dishes.

'Meet you at the pub,' John yelled after him.

Roo came forward, 'Jillian can I send money to my wife with this thing?'

'If she has the same bank and her account is linked to it, yes. Otherwise, you have to do that in the bank.'

Sheepishly Roo asked, 'Could you show me how?' She smiled warmly at him.

'Course! Be with you in a tic - just gotta finish showing the rest of the boys.'

Jillian felt sorry for the men. Twenty years devoid of technology. Their ignorance of so much the world now took for granted made her realize the extent of the sacrifice they had unwittingly made, in trust and loyalty, and how far the wheels of progress had since travelled. These hardened survivors now had to learn the ABC's of the here and now, just to access their well-deserved money. It was an indignity.

The hotel was busy. John found a long table that would cater for everyone. He sat down and discreetly began to look around. Most of the people seemed normal. Some bikers were in the corner, but were keeping to themselves. He moved around the table a little so he could keep an eye on the group.

The rest of his men came in and took seats at the table, the bikies giving each of them the once-over as they did. John nodded in their direction to indicate they wanted no trouble. One ruffian nodded back.

Roo leant forward. 'A few recruits to take on this mission?'

John nodded. 'Could be handy. Probably only good for street fighting.'

Roo laughed. 'Give 'em to me for a few hours. Soon knock 'em into shape. Have 'em hitting target from five hundred in half an hour.'

John ordered ten jugs of beer and a bottle of wine. He paid cash and gave the waitress a ten dollar tip. He looked at Jillian.

'Betcha we're looked after from now on.'

The jugs were soon on the table. John leant over to the waitress with a few folded notes. 'Give those bikies in the corner a couple of jugs will ya?'

She took the money and wandered off. John raised his glass. 'To Delta and all we stand for.'

He leant over to Jillian. 'The mission is on, but if we sniff a double-cross we disappear, never to be seen again.'

Jillian chose not to react. Instead, she lifted her glass. 'Thanks guys.'

John watched with interest when the bikers got their beer, gauging their reaction. The group leader raised his glass. John returned the salute. Then Roo walked over and invited them to join the party. They accepted, and began to drag their table across. John stood up to greet them. He noticed a small patch on the top left of their jackets. "Gulf War Veterans Motor Cycle Club." 'What unit?' he asked.

The leader did something he had not seen for years; shook John's hands clasping them together. He gave the signal of Special Forces.

'SASR,' he said quietly into John's ear. 'And your mob?'

'Strike Force Delta,' John murmured.

They sat down and soon the conversation flowed as freely as the beer. Dicko returned from a trip to the outhouse and went to Bardi.

'Need the bus for a moment. Got some shit to put in it.'

Bardi left with Dicko. They returned half an hour later.

'Should see the shit this old tech-head's got - takes up half the bus!' Bardi said as he sat down.

'You boys got some action going down?' Richard of the Gulf Veterans asked. 'Maybe, you interested?'

'Could be, if the price is right.'

John explained what he knew. Richard listened with great interest.

'We're gonna need quad bikes. I know where I can get at least a dozen of 'em.' 'Re the price - talk to her.' John indicated towards Jillian.

'You're gonna need us John, if what you say is true. I've heard of this NWC mob. They were active in the gulf, razing non-military targets to get the kill rate up. Matter of fact the Special Ops Ranger we worked with sent back data on refugee sites. Next thing, one with more than 500 people in it was liquidated.'

John shot Richard a look that put an end to this conversation. Two police officers had entered the bar. They looked around then walked over, stopping near Bardi..

'What are you doing in here?' one asked, baton in hand. 'Having a beer with my friends Officer,' Bardi replied.

'You know your kind are not allowed in this pub.' Bardi pushed his seat back and stood up.

'What kind is that?' 'Nigger.'

'Jeez, that was close! I'm in the clear. A nigger's a yank. I'm Aboriginal.'

As Bardi began to sit down, the officer struck him on the back with his baton. 'Teach you to be a smart arse, you black bastard.'

Roo shot to his feet, grabbed the law enforcer's baton and began to beat him with it. As his colleague wielded his baton to protect his partner, Richard stood up and gripped it.

'Let the bastard get a lesson.' He stared the officer in the eye.

Roo stopped when the officer dropped to the floor.

'I see or hear you picking on the blacks again, I'll come hunting for you. You have no idea what this man has done for his country, or what he's about to do. You fucking racist piece of white trash! How you got that uniform I will never know.' He turned to the other officer.

'Get him out of here before I turn the boys on you. Don't go telling your boss either. I've got at least thirty witnesses to what you did.'

The second officer nodded, then picked his partner off the floor and helped him out of the bar. 'It's okay mate. We'll get them. I know the community that black is from.'

Richard looked around at the other people in the bar. 'It's all done and dusted. Go back to your drinks.'

John called the young waitress over.

'Could you ask your boss if she has a room for tonight, with one of those spa bath thingies?' She soon returned. 'Yes, we have rooms - would you like to book one?'

'Please. John Kelly's the name' he said, feeling chuffed to be telling it as it was for a change. Richard lent over with a wide grin.

'Isn't that the PM, and is she your spa victim?'.

'Yes, and maybe.' John replied. 'Meet you fellas in the morning, 10 o'clock, first truck bay out of town.' He finished his drink. 'Roo, make sure none of 'em get arrested.'

He and Jillian walked towards Reception. John paid for the room. 'Send up a nice bottle of French Champagne will you please?'

The man smiled. 'Just the one?'

John laughed. 'Bugger it, why not? Make it two. Oh, and one of those seafood platters I saw you serving earlier - with extra crayfish, s'il vous plait.'

Hand in hand, they climbed the stairs to room 11, which was very nice indeed, with king- sized bed, ensuite and a decadently large spa-bath. Only the view was disappointing - the loading yard of a trucking company.

'Hope those buggers won't be loading tonight' John said, pulling down the blind.

Jillian ran the spa, adding a couple of miniature bottles of hotel shampoo. She then sat on the side, watching bubbles froth and foam as the water level rose.

There was a knock at the door. John opened it to receive their midnight feast. He noticed two full crays on the seafood plate.

'You little ripper,' he said, and handed the man a ten dollar note. 'Have one on me mate,' John said, closing the door.

CHAPTER TWENTY-ONE

Hotel Alice Springs

John peeled off his clothing and poured the champagne. When he stepped into the spa and sat down, the water came up to his chest. He patted the seat next to him.

'Coming in?'

Jillian, now in her underwear, raised her glass in a seductive toast. She took a slow sip, "mmm-ed' in appreciation, looked down at John and said

'You don't trust me do you?'

'Sometimes it's hard to tell whose side you're on. Mixed messages. You and Dale plotting our final downfall, so you and your Canberra cronies can go on amassing campaign funds and fuck the rest of the country.'

'Funds keep us in power; we can run ads to counter anything the opposition put up. So yes, I did take the funding offer - until I discovered the real cost.'

'But you're still accepting it?'

'John - I'm a missing person! No doubt the rest of the front bench are still on the take. As long as they stay in power they'll feel untouchable.'

'You know this mission will end your run and bring down the whole deck of cards. So, what would you like to do when it's all over?'

John sipped his champagne, his eyes locked onto the dark patch he could see showing through Jillian's knickers. He could feel himself getting a hard on. The tip of his erection was now showing just above the water.

'Live out my life at Utopia if you'll have me.'

'Darling, you get Frazer's and Charlies in our names and we're in business.'

He stood up and leaned toward her, his head level with her mound of Venus. Arms encircling her thighs, he gently lifted her, inhaling her scent with the same appreciation she'd shown for the champagne, and lowered her into the spa. As Jillian reached over to start the bubble-maker, he eased her knickers down, embracing her from behind. They slipped down into the water and the bubbles covered them.

Jillian was still wrapped around John when he woke next morning. As he kissed her forehead, she stirred a little, her hand tracing its way down and across his body until finding its destination between his legs. She rubbed him gently until he was hard again, then ducked under the covers and began running her tongue over his shaft. It found the head and was soon inside it, the warmth from her mouth flowing over it. She began to suck hard, rubbing her hand up and down the length of him. He pulled her away, turned her onto her back and tasted her salty bush before fully entering her.

Her back arched and moans of pleasure punctuated their age-old dance. John's movements were measured, careful, accurate - every stroke an exploration of length, expertly given. They savoured their primal union, enjoying all the subtleties of familiarity and newness. As Jillian's concentration on his rhythm deepened, her passion mounted. John rode her exhilaration; felt it reaching a crescendo, but delayed the moment his sperm would dart out and be deposited deep into her. His intensity increased - he was not going to miss the moment. Together they finally exploded. He screamed as the fluid darted down his shaft. Her juices oozed onto his groin and the sheets. She closed her vaginal muscles around him, compressing his rod in their mutual ecstasy. Eventually she released him, reluctantly. Locked in each other's arms, joined at hip and lip, they enjoyed the peaceful after-effects of this union, at once thrilling and solacing.

After a mutually deep sleep, John showered, made toast and coffee and brought it to Jillian who was still in bed.

'Come on, we gotta meet the gang soon at the truck stop.'

After breakfast, Jillian went to the bathroom. She took her mobile phone in her toilet bag. After showering, she sent a text. John heard the beep of reply, came in and saw Jillian sitting on the side of the bath-tub, reading the message. He grabbed the phone.

'What the fuck is this thing? You said last night you are behind us. Bullshit! Who are you calling?' he yelled at her.

'Relax!' she countered. 'I texted my secretary to tell her I'm okay. Read the bloody thing if you don't believe me.'

'I would if I knew how to drive one of these things.'

Sheepishly, he handed it back to her. She pulled up the text and showed him. 'See! You have to start trusting people John. You're not in hiding anymore.'

The bus was loaded. John counted over seven boxes stacked at the rear. Stuff bought for the expedition by Dicko, who announced

'Bardi need a hardware-farm shop and some diesel fuel.'

Bardi found a fuel stop and stock agent and parked behind it. John got out and spoke to a storeman.

'You got some bags of urea?'

'Only a few. You're not from round here eh? What you want 'em for?' 'Taking over Frazer's. Need 'em to establish my veggie garden.'

'Got twenty bags. Can spare ten.' John called some of the boys out.

'Load ten,' John said, and went into the store to pay. He pulled out a roll of fifties, 'What's the damage?'

Bardi re-fuelled the bus as John picked up a jerry can and filled it with diesel. He capped it and placed it away from the bags of urea.

'When you're ready Bardi. Don't forget the truck stop.'

Bardi pulled the bus into a line of traffic and headed south. He eased it into top gear and settled down, concentrating on the vehicle in front while still looking out for the truck stop. They found it not far from the outskirts of town.

Richard was the only one there. John and he walked away from the bus to talk.

'Rest of the boys are in town. I gotta go back and give 'em the okay if you still want us on board.'

'Can you get a dozen ATV bikes and bring 'em out?' 'Cost you. Gotta get a truck as well.'

John handed over what reminded of his ten grand withdrawal in Darwin, then walked to the bus, hat in hand.

'Need cash. Large lumps, to iron out some speed humps, chumps. Spare in the hat please ladies and gents.'

Returning, he asked 'Twenty grand ok?' Richard took the money.

'Should get us a good little truck. Where's the delivery place?' 'You know old Frazer's Homestead?'

'Yep, know it well. Did some special ops training out there.'

'See you in two days. Be prepared to be put through your paces. Roo doesn't take on anyone till he's checked 'em out.'

'The PM, is her word good for the two million?'

'I'll back her.' John began to walk back to the bus. Turning, he said 'Two days.'

Frazer's Homestead

The bus was unloaded. Dicko made sure all his boxes were handled with care. He placed them in one pile.

'What the hell've you got here mate?' Bardi asked.

'Well, if this stuff is as good as they reckon, I'll be able to go anyplace on the web; hack into any computer and get all the info John's gonna need. With a bit of tickling up, the two way radios should work in Indigo's black areas as well. At least we'll be able to communicate.

'Smartarse. So that's what you were doing in the electronics shop. Must've cost a packet Dicko.'

'Twenty grand. Gotta pay for quality mate.' He set

'Roo wants me to help with the ring-ins from town. You know, his gut-busting test courses.' 'Hell yeah! His "What doesn't kill ya makes ya stronger" circuit!'

'Does Spider still fuck around makin' stuff from metal?' 'Think so. Ask him –he's over there.' Bardi pointed.

'Hey Spider! Look out - Dicko's got a cunning plan.'

CHAPTER TWENTY-TWO

Frazer's. The Mission Begins.

The early morning sun hung low in the east, casting its reddening light over the land, and making the old homestead appear ghostly. Scrubby trees surrounding the property swayed gently in the breeze. Jillian and John were sitting on the veranda, observing Roo and the men.

'What are they up to?' she asked him.

'Roo is building his infamous "Fucker Course".' 'Please explain!'

John laughed.

'Pre-mission training. Meet his standard or forfeit the mission. He wants to see how these ex SAS boys shape up when they arrive.'

Jillian stood up and took the two coffee cups. 'Just how risky is this mission?'

John looked up at her.

'Same as your party hiding the truth from the people. One slip and it's over. That's why Roo's not taking any chances. He'll train and then retrain. When I get the Intel we'll do mock raids till we have it down pat. Still, there's no guarantee everything'll go our way.'

Dicko had his new toys spread out in logical piles. He had assembled the satellite dish, and tuned it to one of the many out in space, oblivious to which he had locked onto.

Spider was in the shed trying to assemble an item Dicko had drawn up, anxious to meet his exacting standards.

Bardi and his mob came riding in from the community on horses. Dismounting, Bardi addressed John.

'Boss, I can get you two thousand head. The old yards'll need a bit of work.' 'Okay let's do it. How long you need?'

'Give us a week. They'll be as strong as ever.' John patted the horse; he faced Bardi.

'That magic shit you put on your wound, can you get some of it in case we have casualties?' 'Already done Boss, but gotta keep it wet. It's out at the old yards.'

'Good, then they'll be the RV point and the infirmary.'

'So, walla-walla-bing-bang – I get to be the witch-doctor – again!' Bardi said, rolling his eyes.

'That, and Big Chief Cohuna of the advance scouting party. Hope your boys are good on those monsters.' John pointed to the horses.

'My boys want to know if those Rocket Propelled Grenades are to be put in place. It's gonna be hard yakka carrying 'em along with everything else.'

Wait till the SAS boys get here. I want to check this place out with their boss.' Bardi swung himself back into the saddle.

'They're bringing the ATV bikes' 'Better be! I paid for 'em.'

Suddenly, Dicko called John over. Hearing the excitement in his voice, Roo also came running.

'I'm through Boss! Check this out!'

He tapped a few commands into his computer and he was online. 'I can now access any computer in the world that's switched on.'

Dicko was grinning as he demonstrated the surveillance potential of his new toy. 'Oh yeah – get a gander at these too!'

He took one of the boxes and removed a long, silver pencil-like device.

'Laser pointer. Goes out to around five thousand. I'm gonna mount the fifty sniper on a revolving plate, put this little baby on, connect it to my laptop and man! You get a first round hit every time, out to fifteen hundred.'

Roo was impressed.

'Better do some more of that ammo. Any chance you can put those laser pointers on the M16's, and zero them as well?'

'Not a problem. Spider's working on the mounts as we speak.'

'Let me know when you want the weapons for testing.' Roo's excitement was mounting. He swung around to John.

'We've got some good shit on our side if Dicko's dial-up delivers!'

'Roo, those shot guns also have grenade heads. Have the men trained on them, including our SAS boys.'

John walked back towards the house, happy that their plan was taking shape. It was now a waiting game before the recon could begin.

'Hey Bardi, can I borrow two of your horses?'

'No problems Boss!' Bardi yelled from atop his steed.

The Ride

Jillian looked quite the station-hand in her jeans, with a man's shirt tied at the front.

John helped her onto a horse Bardi had said was a quiet one, handpicked for "the missus". They headed north, firstly just walking the hoses. John was in no rush. He observed Jillian in the saddle, she seemed a natural.

'You've ridden before.'

'Well, I grew up on a farm remember. I was horse-mad as a young girl.' They rode up a slight incline. John waited at the top for Jillian to catch him up. Turning to her, he said

'This is what life is about - wide open spaces and not a care in the world.' He pointed to a rocky outcrop.

'Have you ever seen a waterfall in the middle of nowhere?' 'Hmmm - in books maybe...'

'Well, I'm going to show you one where the water is soft and sweet. It falls out of the rock most of the year, encircled by palm trees and other exotic plants. It's where I plan to build Utopia. Come on, I'll show you.'

He urged his horse forward and they tracked their way to the waterfall.

It was spectacular. Tons of water cascaded over high rocks into a pool that spread out over a couple of hundred metres. Lush plant growth had taken hold; it seemed a mini jungle had formed around the waterhole. Jillian sat on her horse in awe. She began to cry. Seeing the tear rolling down her checks, John turned to her.

'You okay?'

'Yep - and now I finally get what you do and why you do it. I got lost along the way, side- tracked from the real world. Locked in a cabinet room making plans for a nation I didn't really appreciate. Caught in the machine.'

'Never too late to put that behind you. Become a normal person again,' John said quietly, not wanting to disturb the tranquillity.

Impulsively, Jillian dismounted, stripped naked and dived into the water hole. The water was cold; a blissful relief from the burning heat of the sun.

'Come on in John, it's heaven.'

Soon he too was in the cool embrace of the water. Jillian swam to where he was standing. 'I never want to leave here John.'

He pointed.

'See those mountains over there? On the other side is our old training ground. That's where the NWC fanatics are doing their thing.'

'Can't we sneak up on 'em and have a look around? She asked 'Not yet. We've got no backup for a recon.'

Just as he finished talking, John heard a thumping noise he was very familiar with. 'Quick, under the trees at the side!' he yelled.

The thumping noise intensified. John wanted to swim back and pull the horses under cover but it was too late.

A reflection from the windshield exposed the chopper, an Apache strike attack with rocket pods and the dreaded 30mm cannon mounted under the pilot. It swung around to face the water hole and hovered for several minutes, scanning the area. Jillian moved a little as the tree branch pushed against her exposed breast. The water suddenly boiled from the chopper's fast firing cannon as it swung left to right over its surface.

John cradled Jillian in his arms as the rounds got closer, pulling her as far as he could into the thick bush that had grown around the water hole. He found the bank and yanked her to land by one hand, just as their hiding place exploded from a missile strike. He pulled her further and further into the bush, knowing the movement detectors on board would have a hard time locating them amid the turbulence of the tree-branches.

John watched in trepidation as repelling ropes were thrown from the side of the chopper and two soldiers began to descend.

'Fuck! The rifle is in the saddle' he exclaimed.

The two soldiers made it to land. One stood guard while the other checked the horses, removing the rifle and throwing it into the spinifex. Systematically, they began to search the area.

John watched. These men were professionals. He heard another sound; a truck grinding its way up the dirt road to the east, then swinging in their direction. Covered in tarps, it stopped about five hundred metres from the chopper. A man stood on the roof of the truck with a shoulder-fired self-propelled rocket. A flash of fire came from the launch tube, and in half a second the chopper exploded in flames. Burning men dropped from the twisted wreck before it slammed into the ground in a ball of fire.

The two that had repelled ran out into the open, and started checking their buddies. The truck advanced, this time with machine guns blasting. It did not take long before the other two men joined their dying comrades.

'Safe to come out now.'

Richard's voice boomed out. John swam to the edge. 'Do you mind? The lady's clothes please.'

He pointed to the pile that had a bra on top. Richard scooped them up and walked to where John was.

'Close shave huh? No sentries, bad move for Special Ops people.' He handed the clothes to John.

'We'll keep cover till you're decent. Better take your own clothes.' He passed the second pile. 'Not good to be caught with your pants down' Richard laughed.

'We got a live one!' one of Richard's men yelled.

'Hog-tie him till we are ready to leave. Keep him alive!' Richard yelled back.

'Hey Adam and Eve, we gotta leave! There's another chopper about fifty out, reckon they got a call.'

Jillian and John appeared, their clothes dripping as they crawled out of the water. 'Who the hell were they?' Jillian was shaken to the core.

'Your daddy's mates,' John replied. 'Come on, before they return.'

Jillian walked to where the horses were tied. She started to cry when she noticed both horses were lying on the ground, their guts protruding from gunshot wounds.

'My God, they've killed Bardi's horses' she said through tears. 'Better them than you my dear,' Richard replied.

'If you're coming, the vehicle's this way.'

They followed him back towards the truck and climbed onto the back. John was astounded at all the weapons - AK47's, SLR rifles and RPG's.

'Where did you get them?' he asked one of the men. 'It's not what ya know mate – it's who ya know.'

Homestead

Bardi approached, looking grim. 'Boss where are my horses?' Gloomily, John dropped the saddles.

'They're dead mate. All we could rescue was the gear.'

'Bugger me. Lend a whitefella your best mounts and this is all he brings back.' Bardi picked up the saddles and carried them away.

'Never again,' he muttered brokenly, walking off. 'My. beautiful bloody horses.' Jillian turned to John. 'The poor man.'

John put his finger to her lips. 'He'll get over it.'

John yelled loud enough so all of Delta Team could hear, including Bardi who was sitting under the tree with the rest of his men,

'First Fucker Training tomorrow. Get a good night's sleep!'

One of Richard's men asked what the fucker course was. John turned and zeroed in on the voice.

'It's the bitch of all courses. Makes the SAS Carter Course look like a walk in the park.'

At sun-up next morning, Roo stood at the front of the house, whistle in hand. He had most of the men in line, though Richard's boys were still getting dressed.

Roo shouted 'Thirty seconds! If you're not out here, your arses are mine.'

Once they arrived, he ordered two ranks, and took the lead, shouting 'Double time!' then set off at a pounding pace.

'We got twenty clicks to march, then repelling, followed by a five click-er with the fifty cal.

After that; five click swim, more repelling and a ten K cool-down,' he barked. 'Come on, step it up you lazy cretins!'

Two hours after reaching the repelling site, they eventually stopped. Allowing them no rest, Roo yelled a scenario.

'You're up here, the weapons you need are down there. The enemy is three clicks behind your sorry arses.'

Roo tied himself onto one of the ropes, and started to go over the side of a nearby cliff. 'Better get cracking! Sniper fire - incoming!' He dropped over the side and ran down the face of the cliff. The rest soon followed. The first man down broke down the heavy machine gun into manageable parts, handing them out as the rest arrived.

'Mortar incoming; move! Move!' he screamed, not giving them a second to catch their breath. Each man took a part of the guns and began to trot off after Roo. The pace was punishing and he knew it. He pushed harder, running back and forward along the line of men.

'Step it out! Move!' he shouted, time and time again, then 'Changed my mind! We do ten clicks with these babies. I've got word some mate's in the shit on top of that hill' he said, pointing to the largest hill on the flat. It looked as if it went straight up in the air for about five hundred feet. Roo was up the hill in a flash. He turned and yelled.

'Get your fucking arses up here, you gutless bunch of old farts!'

Struggling, they eventually made the top. 'Okay, assemble the machine gun!' Roo barked as each team arrived. He went to a rock pile and took out belts of ammo.

'Target Six Hundred - I want it destroyed!' he screamed, pointing to a lonely tree out in the open.

Richard was the first to have his gun chattering. Tracers flew at the target. John was next. Bardi fed in the belt to make sure it didn't jam. John aimed at the base of the tree, sending six hundred rounds a minute down-range into the tree, which soon toppled over.

Roo yelled at Richard 'I said destroy, not just hit the fucking thing! You and your boys got another twenty later this arvo. Okay men, enemy not far! We gotta swim downstream in that river.' He pointed to the white snaking sand in the distance.

'The fifty-cals come along. Let's move it.'

John and Bardi took the weapon between them and trotted off down the hill, the other teams following at point-blank range. Richard made it past John and was at the river first. He told one of the men to grab a log and hold it in the water, then put the machine gun on it, waded in and swam next to it to the end point.

'Fucking smart-arses' John yelled. 'Bardi, log,'

Roo was waiting at the end point. Exhausted, Richard's team pulled themselves from the water and carried the still-dry gun out on its log. John's team was in next. Once on the bank of the river, gun dry, they collapsed. Roo waited till the last team was on dry ground.

'Okay, I lied. We walk back from here. It's only fifteen clicks. A good Sunday walk to get the paper. Pick 'em up and let's get going!'

Roo walked off. One and a half hours later, the men reached the homestead yard. Exhausted, they put the weapons down and sat. Roo appeared.

'Weapons inspection in fifteen. Richard's forward thinking with the log has saved your arse from the run this arvo. Boss debrief now.' He walked to the veranda and waited for John. 'Richard you too.' he yelled at the former SAS leader.

They sat in a small group. 'How did you pull up?' Roo asked Richard.

'Not fucking kidding about the Fucker Course, but overall I think we all did well.'   'Boss?' Roo asked.

'You're an arsehole Roo, but I agree with Richard.'

'Okay, we do it again in two days. From here in every second day we do the Fucker. In between we do a sixteen K forced march.'

'Glad I never joined Strike Command Delta; you pricks are mad!' Richard stood, noticing the twitch in his knee was back.

John laughed. 'Kick your arses any time fella. I want four "away" teams for tomorrow. We do our first recon. Richard, have the bikes off, refuelled and ready. We leave at 0500.'

'Done,' Richard replied.' He walked back to where his men were cleaning the machine guns, sat down and helped out.

John came over and spoke to Bardi.

'You still got our old training maps at your community?' 'Sure have boss.'

'When you've finished, take one of the ATV's and go get them will ya?'

CHAPTER TWENTY-THREE

The ATV bikes were five hundred CC. It gave them plenty of power when needed, and most of all - speed. The men travelled in a V formation to give the best all round protection. Dust billowed from the bikes as they crossed the miles of ground, which was covered in spinifex clumps and trees that had given up the fight to stay standing tall in the harsh environment. The hard sun-baked dirt left little record of the vehicles ever having passed over it.

Roo, John, Max, Bardi and Dicko were Recon Team One, Richard and two of his men along with Fletch - Team Two. The teams swung hard left. John lined up with the southern tip of the ridge ahead. This was the starting point. It also concealed the entrance to the network of caves hidden deep in the sandstone hills which Bardi was going to take them through.

Suddenly, Bardi shot off to the left. John swung his bike to follow and called Roo on the tactical radio.

'Hey my little man, where're you going?'

'Shopping centre,' Bardi replied, as his bike came slowly to a stop. He waited for the others to join him in the tall ghost gums that grew along the sandy river bed, then dismounted, picked some branches and covered his ATV.

'From here on is our sacred place. Everything in the caves is off limits. No touchy touchy, ok? Powerful magic in here. We don't want the Ancestors to make it bad for us. You've gotta promise this - otherwise I can't take you this way.'

The men nodded. 'One soldier to another. God's honour.'

'Good. Cuts off at least two hours footwork going this way, and the Yanks won't know we're in the caves.'

Bardi led the way forward, pushing through the thick small trees that also had a foothold in the river bed that supplied life-giving water. The cave entrance came into view, though the most averred tracker would have missed it. It was hidden behind a large boulder and covered over with thick thorn bushes.

Bardi took a side track and soon the men were standing at the entrance to the caves. 'Those thorns are poisonous' Bardi said. 'Make 'em tea drink and kill ya real quick. See that spider, he good fella, where he is not far from water.'

The men were impressed, learning bushcraft from an expert who had walked the land for years.

Bardi pushed forward, past water trickling down a rock face. Near a small pool, he bent down and picked up a blind snake.

'Him good fella; good tucker as well.'

Putting it down again, he handed John a bush torch and took one himself.

'Here, hand these back.'

He lit his own, touched the others to his and passed them to John.

Sheets of gold veins suddenly appeared in the rocks; nuggets dotted the floor.

'Struth Bardi, you've been holding out on us!' John said, goggling at the pure gold in the rocks. 'This for our kids, so they got something in life. Real bad for white man to take it. Ask that

Lasseter – he found out the hard way. We go on.'

Bardi stepped forward, his torch glowing off the walls of the cave.

Macko, one of the ex-SAS boys, stooped and picked up one of the nuggets.

'Just one won't be missed' he thought. As he stood, a taipan struck. He screamed, and the rest of the men returned.

Bardi made his way back. The man was now laying on the ground in convulsions. 'He take one eh? Bardi checked Macko's pockets, found the nugget and returned it to the ground.

'Told you whitefella's – don't touch nothin' in 'ere. Spirits of elders know - and will protect it.' Richard felt for a pulse. 'He's dead.'

'So would you be; taipan powerful fulla. We leave him here. Good tucker for wild animals 'oo use this place for shelter. Shoulda listened.'

'We can't just leave him here.' Richard interjected. 'Well - you carry 'im, but Spirits won't be 'appy.'

Bardi turned and walked off, saying 'Your choice, SAS.'

Richard put Macko's ground sheet over him. 'Sorry mate.' The group moved off.

The cave narrowed. It was difficult to walk upright. They stooped to pass low hanging rocks. Bardi waited on the other side till they all made it through. Pointing, he said to John 'Out there - flat cliff face, 'e look over that base they built. Good set o' bino's – you can do recon from up 'ere.'

Frazer's Homestead

Jillian came out to where Paterson was. 'So - the Yank's awake?'

Paterson nodded. Time to see what this fella knows.

'Can you get Charlie here? I think he's still sitting under a tree with his mob.'

Jillian nodded and walked toward where the Aboriginals from Bardi's community were sitting. She spoke to Charlie.

'Paterson wants you.'

Charlie walked back with Jillian. 'What he want?'

'He's going to try to get the American from the chopper crash to talk.' Smiling, Charlie stopped her.

'We make him talk, 'ang on.'

Disappearing into the bush, he soon returned with a handful of small seeds. 'Crush 'em missus. Put in 'is drink. 'E talk orright!'

He handed the seeds to Jillian. 'Come on - we go now.'

'Paterson,' she called as she got back. When he approached, she handed him the seeds. 'Crush these and put some in his drink. Charlie reckons it'll make him talk. Says he'll tell all!'

'If he doesn't talk you can eat him Charlie,' Paterson joked. He gave some of the seeds to Jillian.

'Can you crush these? I'll get him onto the veranda and see what he knows. Grab a pad and pencil so you can write down what he says.' Paterson snickered. 'Hope John can spare a bottle of Scotch for these babies' he said, smiling at the "magic beans" in his hand.

Cliff- face Overlooking Camp Indigo

John and Richard both lay flat, binoculars scanning the base. John noticed the five ICBM rockets. Standing tall near what appeared to be launch towers. Fuel lines were connected. He scanned the camp, identifying seven trident missiles. 'Why seven?' he wondered, then lowered his binoculars.

'What the fuck? They're going to start World War Three with all that shit.'

'Dunno - but it doesn't look good,' Richard replied, still surveying the camp. He pointed. 'The building at the front looks like the guard house.'

John took a look.

'Yep I agree. Where the hell is the control room? They must have one for those missiles?'

'That my friend is the large building, the tin one with all those air conditioners coming out of the walls. Next to that is the generator room.'

'Okay, do a mud-map with your estimates of distance. Reckon we can take down those ICBM's?' John asked.

'Not easy. We'd need to have the explosive under them. That means getting into the compound. Big risk. But the Tridents, we can take them out with RPG's from this distance.'

Dicko came back out and lay down near Richard. 'Found the control room?'

'Yep - it's that big silver tin place.' Richard pointed.

'May I?' he pointed to the binoculars. Taking them, Dicko honed in on the building until he found what he was looking for. 'Just as I figured.'

'Figured what, brains?' Richard asked

'Well, you know as well as I do; electrical radios and such don't seem to work in the valley. Something to do with a presumed planet strike eons ago. That tells me every signal is by wire, which'd include satellite info they'd need. So my guess is – there's a junction dish outside the valley. If we can find it, I'll tap into it and wreak havoc with the computer systems that drive those ICBM's.'

John looked over. 'Okay, we go looking. Do you know what we are looking for?'

'Not really, but it'll have a dish and a distribution box of some kind, with live wires in a cable heading to the base camp.'

'Okay. I've seen enough. Let's get out of here,' John said, giving the signal for the men to head back into the caves. Macko's body was no longer lying where they had left it.

Bardi came over to Richard.

'He tucker now - part of this country. His spirit'll live 'ere forever. He'll become one of the protectors, along with my ancestors.'

Frazer's Homestead

'You get all that down?' Paterson asked, half propping up the now very drugged and drunk Yank.

'Every word. My God! If it's true, Australia is done for' Jillian said.

'Yep, not to mention the Middle East. Millions of bloody people and further strikes on random capitals until the world agrees to abide by NWC rules. Like having a loaded gun at your head with someone pulling the trigger back - just waiting for the bang.'

'One you'll never hear.' Jillian wept. 'How the hell did I get sucked into dad's crooked lease deal? God, my country faces war with the US! Paterson, what are we gunna do?'

She cried on his shoulder.

The Dish

Dicko spotted it hidden in a small valley. He raced his ATV to the location and was soon inspecting the set up. The junction box was not even locked. He opened it. There was a USB port wired directly to the hard drive. He smiled.

'Candy from a baby!'

Closing the box, he stated 'It's do-able Boss.' 'Ok - get your tools, Bardi, go with him.'

John pushed on, making his way to the cattle yards. Bardi's mob were skilfully installing rails and extending the yard to hold two thousand head.

'What the hell has this got to do with our mission?' Richard asked.

John laughed. 'You've got a movement sensor and they all go off. What would you think is happening, and what would you do?'

'Massive invasion. Call out the guard. Get the soldiers to battle stations.' Exactly, but they're going to be chasing cows, not us' John laughed. 'You're a sneaky bastard Kelly,' Richard said.

'Must be my convict streak' John replied, getting back on his ATV. 'Come on, let's go home and put what we know into a plan.'

Frazer's Homestead

'For fuck sake, shut up!' Paterson yelled at the Yank, who was still running off at the mouth.

Charlie came over.

'You give 'im too mucha that stuff; 'e talkie-talk all night now.'

Paterson looked up as the ATV's roared into the yard, dust billowing around the riders as they pulled to a stop. Jillian ran out to meet them. She hugged John.

'We have to stop them John!,' she insisted, in anguished tones. 'What are you on about?'

'All the Aussie capitals are going to be hit with nerve gas. It'll kill millions. He... he told us.

Paterson gave him some truth powder and he confessed everything.'

'Settle down and start from the beginning,' John said consolingly, putting his arm around Jillian and walking her back to the old homestead.

Paterson, what's she on about?' he asked, making the veranda.

Paterson started to explain. 'We've got massive problems if what that Yank said is true. It'll be ICBM's for the Middle East, Trident's for Australia, and gassing cities at random all around the world to force the rest of the world to conform to their law.'

'Well, that explains the seven Tridents. One for each Capital on the mainland.'

John took a drink of water offered by Jillian.

'Do we know when all this is supposed to happen?' Jillian grabbed her notes.

'16th of June.' She handed them to John. 'I wrote down everything he said.' 'You're getting the hang of all this' he said, smiling warmly at her.

'Did Dicko and Bardi come back?'

'Yep, He grabbed his computer and took off.'

'Okay, let's wait till Dicko reports back and see what he's got. Between his info and the Yanks, we should have a much clearer picture. Hmmm – only six days till D-day. Roo, crank up the training. More in weapons if we can spare the ammo. I want first round sniper hits at one thousand, no excuses. Max, work your magic with that urea and diesel. We need at least enough to bring down the western wall of the canyon. Richard, do what you do best. Recon. ATV's. I don't care how little you get, but get it. Jillian, when Dicko returns, help him out on the computer. Spider, you and I are going to do a little hunting. We need fresh meat to feed this mob. I saw a bunch of 'roos over near Well 5.'

As the team went about their assigned tasks, John and Spider climbed into one of the four wheel drive utes. Richard approached them.

'Here, take this.' He handed John an SLR assault rifle. 'Better than that M16 ya got.' He grinned and gunned the engine of his ATV, taking off in a cloud of dust, his team falling in behind.

Jillian waved goodbye as John and Spider headed out to Well 5.

Satellite Receiver Point and Junction Box.

Bardi followed orders, with no idea of what was going on. He watched with interest as Dicko plugged into what he thought was a telephone line.

'So - you can tell what they up to by that wire?'

'Yep. If I can crack the code I'll be able to get into the main frame and find all sorts of goodies.'

'Bullshit! With a puckin typewriter?' Bardi was scornful.

'It's a computer mate. Works wonders if ya know how to use it.'

'Nah, gimme a telephone any day. Least I know 'oo I'm talkin' to. I'm goin' up the 'ill a bit; keep an eye out.' Bardi grabbed his M16 and took off.

Well 5

The Apache hung in the sky like a giant Eagle hovering over its intended kill, its side bulking with rocket pods. Sunlight reflected off its clear Perspex windshield, masking the dark outline of two pilots. Heat shimmers danced from the ground below.

The mob of kangaroo's sensed the threat and took flight before it had a chance to strike.

Spider looked up from his shooting place as the Apache dipped its nose and inched forward. The cannons on the front surveyed the landscape, barrels sweeping the spot where Spider had been observing the Kangaroos.

John had the hard-hitting Self Loading Rifle in his hands. He pointed it in the direction of the beast. It fell into his site picture; all he had to do was squeeze the trigger and send thirty rounds of 7.62 bullets slamming into the helicopter. His finger tightened. He tucked the weapon into his shoulder. His thumb flicked the safety off. He squeezed and felt the bolt slam forward, then nothing. The rifle had misfired.

The hovering monster of death suddenly thundered away, passing right over where John and Spider had lain in wait for their kill.

John's face broke into a cold sweat. If the gun had fired he would have exposed their position. He and Spider would most likely be a pile of mincemeat. He lay still, heart palpitating, chin still resting on the rifle.

Carefully, Spider made his way to John.

'Boss, those choppers gettin' more'n'more. Reckon they know we're here, lookin' for 'em? Maybe the three fellas we stripped back at the waterhole made it back in one piece.'

'The homestead! The chopper headed in that direction,' he screamed. 'SHIT! Let's go!' Running to the ute, John grabbed the radio.

'Recon One, return to base camp, with caution, NOW! Apache heading in that direction. ' The ute flew over the ground, and the riders didn't waste time on the rough ground. John could see a dust trail to the south.

'Recon One; Max! You on channel?' he screamed over the radio. 'Roger.' Max's voice came over the speaker.

'Get under cover! Incoming Apache.'

John and Spider made it back just as the Apache turned to fire on the old homestead. Out of the corner of his eye, John saw Richard and his boys roaring in. The chopper flew straight over the house, then John heard the sound of its turbine engine, coughing. The Apache was in trouble. It began to descend.

The ATV's headed to where it was putting down and screeched to a stop. Richard and his crew aimed their AK47's at the chopper and its crew, who gave up without a fight and came out, hands on heads. They were soon disarmed.

John made it over in the ute. 'Put 'em on the back,' he ordered. The four American crew were soon loaded, along with an armed guard. John drove them back to the homestead, not knowing exactly where he was going to put them. The ATV's stopped right behind the ute. Richard's team levelled their rifles at the captives.

Quickly, John made his way to the rear, his own rifle in the ready position. He eyed off the prisoners as they clambered down, pulling one of them aside. He recognised the man. 'You!' he barked at a tallish man displaying Master Sergeant Stripes on his uniform.

'I fucking know you! You were on Devils. Hey boys, guess who we just captured?'

Max, Roo and Fletch came over to look the man in the eyes. He had masterminded the "spin" about the President's downed chopper, shifting the blame onto Delta Team.

'Well I'll be buggered,' Fletch said eventually. 'Sergeant Pillman. It's been a long time no see.' He leant forward. 'You're dead, fucker.' He spat in the man's face.

Richard came over. 'Pillman! Remember me, you fucking arse? You ordered the strike in Kuwait that killed five hundred refugees.'

Richard swung his fist hard, hitting Pillman in the side of the face and knocking him to the ground.

'Come on tough man, get up.'

John intervened. 'He's worth more alive than with his brains splattered all over this red dirt.' 'Tell that to the five hundred he murdered.' Richard kicked dust into Pillman's face.

John pulled him to his feet

'I should let the men tear you limb from limb you piece of shit.'

He pushed him in the direction of the house. The old cool-room would have to double as a jail for now.

Un-expectantly, Pillman leered 'Kelly, you'll be kissing my feet when our task is done. Hardest thing I have to think about is which Australian city I'm gonna take over. Brisbane, I reckon. Golden beaches, chicks that make you want to cum in your pants. Yep, Brisbane. I've got first choice y'know.'

'Gunna be hard doing that from an unmarked grave in the middle of the Australian desert.

Get in there!'

He pushed his adversary into the cool-room and pulled the door closed, slipping the bolt lock over, then returned to oversee the team.

'Richard, see what these three scumbags know, then lock 'em up with that other dog turd in the cool room.'

Richard cracked his knuckles. 'My pleasure.'

'Make sure they have a face left,' John replied. 'Where the hell are Bardi and Dicko?'

He was worried. Darkness was approaching stealthily. The hills in the distance showed only a soft red glow from their apex as the sun lowered in the west. Eventually he heard the sound he'd been hoping for - the ATV returning with Dicko and Bardi.

Garth returned from the chopper site, looking grim.

'Better have sentries out tonight, that chopper has a locator beacon going like there's no tomorrow.'

The generator was labouring; John turned and noticed the landing light to the small airstrip come on.

'Who the fuck is this?'

Garth looked skywards.

'Bugger me! It's Doc Brain's plane. How the hell does he know where we are?'

'Who gives a shit? He's back! The team's together again. Take a vehicle and go get the bastard.'

John jumped with joy, yelling as Bardi and Dicko pulled to a stop. 'Doc's here boys!' he shouted, pointing to the airstrip.

Bardi grinned. 'Hooray! I don't have to play doctor anymore. You bloody beauty.' When Doc climbed out of the ute, he yelled to John who was sitting on the veranda,

'This better be the real thing! Fucking Dicko sent me an email saying it was urgent,' 'Nice to see you too Doc,' John said, taking two cans of beer from the small car fridge at his side. He tossed one to Doc.

'Take it you still drink beer, or are you a whisky man now?'

'Beer's fine. How the fuck are you? Are all the boys here? Where's that big Bardi fucker?' 'Shit, you wanna know a lot, don't ya?'

John laughed and put his hand out to the man who had dug many a bullet out of him.

'I got a locator signal coming in. Is there a plane crash or something?' Doc asked. 'Nope, not a plane.' John pointed to the Apache. 'One of them. Seemed to have a bung engine just as it was about to let loose on the house. Got Pillman locked up inside as we speak.' 'Pillman! That name still sends shivers over me. He's here?'

'Yep, we've got him. Turns out your old mate Taylor is the Base Commander. He is a two star general now.'

'I should've put sleeping juice in him when I worked on his sorry arse on Devils. He is one mad man John, a real split personality disorder I reckon.'

'You said it. He's now playing God, with five ICBM's and seven Tridents.'

'Jeez! That's a lot of fire power for someone who's holding the winning cards right now.' 'Not for long mate. We've got a plan in the works. Are you in?'

'I'm here aren't I?'

Doc looked at the homestead; he had once used it as a first aid station when the Delta boys trained at Indigo.

'The old place is in need of a few repairs from the last time I was here.' 'Over twenty years it's been a long time Doc.' John said.

'Cripes! That long?' He looked at the building again. Jillian walked out and over to where John was sitting.

'Who's the gorgeous creature? Shit, it's the Prime Minister. Sorry about that!'

'I'll take it as a compliment Doctor.' Jillian replied grinning. She turned to John. 'Dicko and I have printed off his findings. I think you'd better have a look.'

Reading realization dawned on John.

CHAPTER TWENTY-FOUR

The Choppers Arrive at Frazer's

Two more Apache attack helicopters came from out of nowhere. John shoved Jillian into the house and then pulled Doc to the ground.

The ground in front of the homestead erupted in dust and flying rocks from the 30mm cannon fire. Bullets struck the stone buildings; large shales of rock were ripped from the stones and flung around like colliding meteorites. Dust and chips of rock flew over Doc's and John's heads and bodies as they lay flat on the veranda floor.

John heard Jillian scream. He crawled to the door; she was lying in a pool of blood. A shard of rock had hit her in the back and she was not moving.

'Medic!' John screamed.

Dicko came running out. He helped Doc pull her out of the line of fire into the next room.

John made it to one of the utes that had a mounted fifty cal. He loaded a 200-round belt of ammo and swung it around towards the lead chopper. His finger never released the firing lever until the breechblock slammed on an empty chamber. The barrel was glowing red. He put in another belt and cranked the cocking-lever back. He aimed; waited. The lead chopper exploded into flames. The other chopper turned away and disappeared into the night sky.

John ran back to the house. He saw the blood trail where Jillian had been dragged. He came to the door; Paterson and Dicko stopped him.

'Just let Doc do his stuff Boss. She's in good hands.'

Spider staggered in. The bottom of his left leg was gone. He fell forward onto the floor. Dicko and Paterson hurried over and began field first aid till the blood flow began to slow. Richard ran in.

'I've got wounded out here!' he screamed. 'We need a medic - gut wound.'

Doc heard, but kept working on Jillian. Then he stopped, knowing he should tend to the worst wounded first.

'Triage,' he said to himself.

'Paterson, get in here! Hold that towel on the wound; use pressure.' He ran to the front of the house.

'Where's the gut wound?' he barked at Richard, not knowing who the man was.

Richard pointed to a man lying on the veranda. 'Do your best, Doc - he's got a wife and kids.'

Doc looked grimly at the prone figure, then checked his vitals. He closed the man's eyes and stood up.

'Sorry mate - your bloke didn't make it. Where are the others?' Richard stood stunned.

'The others, son!' Doc yelled.

'Guy over here in the bushes; got a lump of chopper in his leg.'

Doc followed Richard to where the man was. The leg was a mess. A part of the tail rotor had lodged in his thigh. Uncovering the wound, Doc observed the man's hip had been smashed into pulp by the rotor part. It would only be a matter of time before he bled out.

'Nothing I can do for him. He needs major surgery. His hip's in a thousand bits.' 'Morphine?' Richard asked.

Doc handed over the syringe.

'You better take the bottle as well soldier.'

Doc knew exactly what Richard was about to do - the kindest thing under the circumstances. 'I'll stay with him till its time' Richard said sadly. 'You've got others to treat Doc. Thanks for understanding.'

Doc walked away. He could hear Richard praying

'Yea, though I walk through the valley of the shadow of death, I will fear no evil.' Doc looked at Spider's wound next.

'Sorry mate – you'll need a prosthetic limb from here on in. Good news is - they're bloody bionic now eh?'

Spider gripped Doc. 'Can't you fix it?'

'Not this time mate. It's shattered. The bottom of your leg is most likely outside in half a dozen pieces. All I can do now is stop blood-loss and patch it over. You know battle surgery.'

Spider nodded. 'Knock me out cold though won't ya? Go save the PM.'

Doc spent another two hours treating Jillian, emerging in a sombre mood. He walked over to John.

'She's resting, but she needs immediate evacuation to a hospital John. Her back's damaged.' 'Bardi's bush medicine; we can try that' John suggested.

'Witchcraft John,' Doc countered, shaking his head.

'No. I've seen it in action, it works. Two months ago, Bardi was about to lose his leg. Check him out. Notice him limping; infected?'

'Up to you and her John. Worth a crack if there's no alternative. I have another patient, best of luck.'

Doc headed back toward Spider , then turned.

'You really think Bardi's stuff works? Ok - before we try it on the PM, let's give Spider some. He's going to lose his leg and I'm not sure there's enough skin cover the wound.'

'Ask him then' John replied.

Richard appeared, looking worse for wear.

'We've gotta move these people in the next 48 hours! They know where we are and it won't be long before they use this place as target practice.'

'Mate, move the PM over rough terrain and she'll be in a wheelchair for the rest of her life' Doc re-enforced the danger.

Bardi returned with a Mona Lisa smile. He had the plants and his grey "mud." Taking over the makeshift kitchen, he brewed the roots of the plants, waited for the liquid to cool, then added it to his mud.

'Okay Doc, it's ready.'

He took the first dose in to Spider.

'Keep him talking. Tell him I'm flushing the wound or something.'

Bardi gently poured the liquid into the open wound, then covered it with the mud. 'Now we wait and see. Next - PM?'

'Not till I know it works. How long will it take on Spider?' 'Twelve, maybe twenty four hours.'

'Then we wait. There's enough pain relief to last,' Doc said.

Dicko came out, looking serious. He addressed John.

'Boss, need to see you. How would you like to end all this without anyone getting killed?' 'As a commander that'd be a dream outcome, but it's not going to happen.'

'Maybe it can.' Dicko held up his laptop. 'So how do you propose to do it?'

'Change the destinations of the ICBMs and the Tridents.'

'Good idea, but they'll change 'em back, then we're back at square one.'

Dicko fired up his laptop and entered the command for the Indigo site. He grinned slyly at John.

'Administrator's password. I can change anything on the database; block any changes. Disable latitude and longitude coordinates for the missiles. I could make those Tridents gain altitude to a thousand metres then turn and come straight back down on the base.'

John looked impressed. He stroked his chin.

'I think I'm getting the picture. Ok - look up the coordinates for Washington, New York CBD, Dallas, Chicago and Newport. See how they like getting their own hardware back. You don't reckon I can make a phone call on that do you?'

'Only to lines within the base.'

'That'll do nicely. Email the base commander. Tell him I have four of his men and any strike on the homestead will result in their death. Sign it with my name. Yes?'

'Not a problem Boss. While I'm at it I'll change the master password so they can't delete us from the system.'

'Do it, and relocate those missiles to the new destinations, Tridents as well. See if he thinks I'm bluffing. Can we get the President on that?'

'He's just a click away Boss.'

John looked for Roo; he was outside cleaning the weapons.

'Get those rockets in place at the caves; the fifties and whatever else you think we'll need. Tell Richard to have his men on 20-minutes-to-move notice.

'Dicko'll tell you about his thing?'

'Yep. That's our back-up plan. I'm not putting all my eggs in the technology basket.

Computers can't plan a war or fire a rifle.'

CHAPTER TWENTY-FIVE

President Philips was in the Oval Office. He looked over at the gifts given to the US by other countries. He particularly liked the stuffed kangaroo from Australia. Amazing strength in this animal's hind legs.

When Peter Miller the Secretary of Defence came in, he immediately regretted interrupting the President's cherished quiet time. Time to sit and ponder his dominion of the best military in the world, and how one word from him could bring a nation to its knees. He looked up.

'Peter! Come in, take a seat.'

Placing a folder on the President's desk, Miller said

'This is a "courtesy" email just dispatched from one John Kelly in Australia. The game's up Sir.'

Flicking the folder open to read its contents, the President replied

'First, this is not a game. Second, what's happened to our premier hitman? Your task was to dispatch them to take care of this piece of shit. What happened?'

'They're on their way as we speak; my Intel has them touching down in Perth right about,' he looked at his wrist watch, 'now.' A light aircraft is waiting to take them to Indigo by night's end.'

'So how is the game up my friend?'

'Kelly has locked us out of the control computer; changed the launch longitudes and latitudes. We push the button and five ICBM's will head for the states. He has fucking locked us out.'

'Smartass. I'd do the same. Does the Indigo Base Commander know where this rat is?' demanded the President with agitation, swivelling in his chair.

'Yes Sir, an abandoned ranch called Frazer's, about fifty miles from the base.' 'Well level the fucking place.'

'He has four of ours as prisoners.'

'Look Peter, we're in the business of fixing the over-population of this world. Count the four as victims along with Kelly's men. Get onto it.'

'Sir,' Peter tried to argue. 'The discussion is closed.'

Peter walked to the door. Turning, he said 'One of the prisoners is your grandson.'

He walked back to his office and called Brain and Douglas, the two ex-navy Seals he had dispatched for the hit. He was just about to hang up when Brian eventually answers his mobile. 'Brian, it appears that the President's grandson is being held at Frazer's. Bring him back alive.' 'Email me the latest Intel on the target.'

Brian hung up and the men moved forward in the line to customs clearance. They took a taxi to the designated motel, booked in then found a place to eat. Doug ordered beers, unaware of the potency of full strength Australian lager. Soon both men were drunk. A waiter tersely asked both men to leave under threat of being removed by the police. Brian threw a fifty dollar note onto the floor as they walked out.

'Let's grab a cab man! Driver – casino! Take these Seals to the roulette wheels!'

The sun was shining on the casino carpark when Brian opened his eyes. His shoulder ached like it was on fire. Doug was lying next to a car nearby, his head smashed in and a knife sticking out of his gut. Brian crawled over and checked his pockets. The five thousand dollars was gone. He was now alone and broke; their remaining money was in the motel safe.

Frazer's

John stopped near Dicko.

'Any word from the President?'

'Not yet, but the Base Commander wrote back; two words: "Bull Shit.' 'Never figured Mike Taylor'd come back with anything else.'

'That the same Taylor from Devils?'

'The very same. Where Pillman is, Taylor is.' 'What now?'

John walked around, unsure, but knowing something would come to him soon. 'Gotta think on that one.'

Doc came in, looking incredulous.

'Gotta bottle this shit! It's bigger than Bex! Spider's leg has demonstrated definite and rapid repair, and the PM's also showing signs of making a full recovery. This deepest cut of all is that now I'll have to apologise to Bardi Yowch!'

'Justice, Doc.'

Doc walked off muttering to himself. He stopped at the scotch bottle and took a swig. 'I still can't believe it. Weeds and mud - bloody impossible.'

He turned and walked back to John.

'Forgot to tell you; I think she is in the pudding club. Laugh that off funny man.'

'Owe my god, a child and I will be able to raise it...You fucking ripper' John stood chest out and smiling. 'Well that's it Doc, we move to Charlie's Hut first light. Dicko, tell the boys. My guess is this place will be a pile of rocks by tomorrow night.'

John went to find Jillian, who looked up at him with slightly nervous anticipation. He kissed her cheek.

'Well, well. A little brother or sister for young John eh?'

She smiled in relief, and they embraced. 'Its not definite John, but yes it is rather exciting. How are you feeling?' he asked.

'Good! Not tempted to walk yet, but I reckon I could. Doc said to give it another twelve hours.'

'We're gunna have to bail out of here. Got a feeling they'll level this place tomorrow, You up to moving?'

'Well I'm not sticking around to be bombed into oblivion. Can't you guys stop this madness?'

'Giving it our best shot.' She rolled onto her side. 'How's Spider?'

'Lost his leg from the knee down. Max and the boys are with him now.

Jillian gripped his hand and squeezed it.

'You have a great bunch of men John. I can see why you're all so close.'

'Yep. Goes way beyond friendship now. We're brothers. They'll help build our Utopia – you'll see.'

'So I might be carrying the first Utopian child?'

'You said it, and there'll be lots more when the boys get their wives and girlfriends here. I've gotta go and put things in place. See ya later.'

John kissed her again, and left the room, chest out and walking tall. He approached Dicko, who was still at his computer.

'Can you show me how to use this thing? I need to talk to the Base Commander.'

'Whoa! The great John Kelly is coming into the 21st century! Ok, I'll set up a Live Chat. Just type. He'll see your writing in a few seconds.'

'Ok, but stick around. I'm crap at typing.'

Dicko established Live Chat in a twinkling, and called John over. 'He's accepted – wanna use video as well?'

'You serious?' John's eyebrows rose.

'Yep – Skype is two-way. You can see him and he can see you.'

The screen on the computer changed. In one corner John could see his own image, then Mike Taylor appeared.

"Well Mr Kelly. It's been a long time." "Mike! Three Stars now. Congratulations." "What do ya want?" Taylor asked.

"An answer. Why are you targeting Australia?"

"Well John, there's lots of things we need. And you have 'em! Can' t see that you're just gunna hand it over so - NWC's gunna take 'em."

"And that's the plan for the rest of the world as well, eh? With Australia the first to see how your gas works?"

"Still the smart-ass you were on Devil's, Kelly? Pity your little trick with the rockets didn't work. You can tell your computer man our problem's almost fixed. We'll be back online before those birds are ready to fly. As one officer to another, I suggest you fly the white flag. There's two tank troops heading your way fully loaded with HE. Catch ya later John."

The screen went blank.

Dicko instantly flicked into a different screen.

'He has one Trident back online and it's in countdown. I can't reverse that - it locks everyone out during countdown.'

'How long before it flies?' 'Twenty-three hours Sir.'

'The smart basted. Keep trying to get them back into your control'

John went outside to enjoy the sunset. The sky was crimson, with pink-flamingo clouds fleeing over the small hills in the distance. Patch was looking over the helicopter that had run out of juice.

'All it needs is gas Sir. It'll fly like a bird again.'

'See if Bardi can get some through his community. Can you fly it?' 'A chopper's a chopper Sir.'

'Have the boys taken the rocket and other the supplies to the cave?' 'Far as I know. Gonna tinker some more on the bird if that's okay.'

'Hey Dicko!' John yelled. 'Worked out the fifty cal fire ring system yet?' 'Yep. Roo tested it this morning. Works like a dream.'

'Max! We move in the morning.'

'If there is anything left of this place,' he said to himself.

The sun had sunk a little further. John took a can of beer from the small fridge and ripped the top back. He closed his eyes, imagining life in Utopia.

How much easier it would be with no-one telling them what they could and couldn't do, or taking money and calling it income tax.

He opened his eyes and looked out over the barren plains, envisaging the nice house he'd build Jillian and their bundle of life near the waterhole. Soon.

Spider hobbled out on a crutch, Jillian at his side. 'Come to say thanks Boss.'

'Save it for Bardi. It was his bush medicine that saved your life mate.'

CHAPTER TWENTY-SIX

Richard knew they had but one shot to bring down the Trident missiles if Australia was to be saved. The equipment was in place. He double checked each position.

John had inserted detonators for a controlled explosion. He ran the wires back to his hideout and left them near the detonation device. He was ready.

Roo, Max and Paterson made it to the compound fence. They had noticed movement detectors but with prior knowledge of the valley, managed to avoid them. Five ICBM missiles stood tall. The markings of the USA had been removed and a symbol of a clenched fist had been painted on the side.

Roo inched forward to get a better view, slipping into the cavity behind a pile of discarded pallets. One of the NWC security guards was doing his rounds. Roo's AK 47 was at the ready, though he did not like this weapon; it was inaccurate and wasted bullets. His preferred rifle was the self-loading 7.62 that was discarded as the mainstream weapon in the eighties. He so wished he had one in his hands right now.

The security guard walked close to the pallets. He turned to walk behind them, which would expose Roo's position. Paterson saw what was going on. He inched his crossbow out, affixed a sleeping tip, aimed through the telescopic sight and fired. The guard was hit in the middle of his back and fell silently to the ground. Roo quickly dragged the body out of view of any other security patrols.

Paterson moved forward and joined Roo.

'You see any more?' he whispered to the man he most admired as a battlefield-hardened NCO. 'Reckon if we plant the explosive to topple that one,' Roo said, pointing to the first and closest missile, 'we can use it to bring the others down?'

'Nup. It'll miss 'em by a good ten feet Roo. Besides, they're filled with that nerve agent shit. We won't get ten feet. I think we use the patch explosive so when they get to two grand in the air it goes bang. Hasn't Dicko changed the launch codes or something?'

'Supposed to have, but John thinks that prick running the show here has accessed and changed them back. Dicko's not sure if he has the time after launch to redo his thing.'

'Shit!' Paterson retorted. 'That means we've gotta bring 'em down.'

'About the size of it Paterson. Stay here; I'm gonna try to get Dicko on the radio - see what he's up to.'

Roo slithered back to where the others were waiting.

'Get Dicko on the eau de cologne!'

Patch finished fuelling the killing machine, then climbed into the cockpit and sat looking at the array of switches and dials confronting him. This was far more advanced then the Jet Ranger he was used to flying.

'Well, if they can teach a dumb-arse Yank, I can fly this,' he said to himself, twisting knobs and flicking switches. Patch searched the dash but could not identify anything that resembled a starter switch. His thumb brushed a button on the stick between his legs and the blades began to whine.

'What a fucking stupid place to put that.'

Patch hit it again and held it down. He grinned to himself as the burners cut in and the turbine began to whine. As the blades thumped the air, he gripped the selective, twisted the power on and gently pulled back on the control. Slowly, the beast lifted. He landed and lifted again, allowing himself enough height to test the sensitivity of the controls, which were very light and extremely responsive. Finally, he touched down and switched it off, then sat looking at the remaining dials, taking in what they did and how they worked. The Weapon Selector screen was clearly marked.

He now placed the remainder of the two hundred litres of fuel into the beast and topped the tank up from the second two hundred litre drum.

Meanwhile, Bardi briefed the men that the cattle he'd penned earlier would soon be stampeding down the valley to set off the enemy's hundreds of movement sensors.

'They'll come out shooting, so make sure you stop near the big trees at the river bed,' he insisted.

Indigo Base Camp

Roo pulled the team back well away from the fence. They hid under a clump of tee-trees.

'He needs height and lots of it to access the missiles. Shit. The highest hill around here tops out at five hundred.'

'Doc's plane, we can use that,' Max said, grinning.

'If that tin pot thing can get up high enough,' Roo replied, shaking his head. 'Come on, we gotta figure out a way to bring 'em down.'

'Got it!' Paterson announced. 'Fifty cal, all with trace. We hit the fuel tanks and bring 'em down. The fire should neutralise the gas; at least that's what my NBC instructor in the army told me.'

'Yep, we can hit 'em from where Richard and his team are. Let's get it organised. Hang on, how far do you think those missile are away?' Roo asked.

'Two hundred tops, why?' Paterson replied.

'Well from here we've got just the thing. Let's get cracking.'

Frazer's

John returned filthy, mud on his face; clothes ripped. 'Looks like you've had fun,' Jillian commented. 'It's all ready for tomorrow. You coming out?'

'Not going to stay here and go down with the building! While I'm on that point - what are you going to do with them?'

Jillian pointed to where the American's were being held. 'Far as I am concerned they can get buried in this place.' 'That's murder John.'

'And plastering nerve agent all over the Middle East and our own capital cities isn't?' 'Point taken, but I still think it's wrong.'

'Jillian, if they had our son and you knew he'd be killed in this confrontation, what would you do, even if you had the means to destroy?'

'Hold off! What are you saying?'

'The chopper pilot is the grandson of the US President. I don't think they'll flatten this place.

Not till they're sure he won't be a casualty.' 'How long have you known?'

'From the time we caught 'em. Been using him as my trump card. Commander's prerogative.'

'Well Patch finally got that chopper running so... why can't we just fly out of here and leave it to our soldiers to take care of?'

'Because we got invited to this party. You held up your end, so we see it through. That's our code. Besides, by the time the serving SAS get here, those rockets will be high over the Middle East and all our capital cities will be in the firing line. I've got nothing against Mr Joe Blow on the street; only with the select few who did this to us.'

'My father?'

'Yep. He's one of 'em.'

'And his daughter...where does she fit in?'

'She didn't do anything, so I've got nothing against her.'

John walked over and cuddled her. 'Besides, I love her very much.' Darwin

Brian Tanner sat reading a newspaper in Arrivals. When Flight 95 from America had arrived and cleared customs, he got up, straightened his shirt and walked to the security gate. Todd came out followed by Ryan and Skip.

'Soon as you get your bags we're on our way to Indigo. We have to do it tonight.' The other nodded. 'Everything organised?'

'Yes, weapons and all. They're waiting for us at Indigo.'

Brian took the men over to the domestic airport where a charter pilot was waiting to fly them to Indigo.

'This place you want to go, you know it is designated military?'

'She's jake mate - we still go. It's now under lease by the Yanks. Here's the frequency you can contact them on.'

'Okay, you're paying the bill. Which reminds me; five G's up front.' Tanner handed over the money. 'Let's get your bucket of bolts in the air.'

Frazer's

John listened. This noise he had heard many times. It still sent a chill through his body. The sound of steel tank tracks grinding the ground into dust.

'I'll be behind the house hill,' Richard remarked.

Thunder cracked in the sky, and both men jumped, thinking it was the first round of many to come. The sky opened, loosing torrents of rain. Lightning punctuated the long storm cloud covering the entire area.

'Hope these wankie yankee tankies know it's black soil plains in this neck o' the woods.

Sink down to the top tracks they will.' John gave a little laugh.

'How far away do you think they are?' Richard asked, sipping his beer.

'Five, maybe six clicks.'

'Well they won't open up yet. Never known a yank tank commander to do indirect fire. He prefers direct so he can correct properly. Black soil huh? How long before this rain starts it off?'

'Twenty minutes at this rate.' 'Time for another beer.'

Richard handed John another can and took one for himself.

'I'm gunna post some boys out tonight. Maybe even send an away team to have a wee look at those tanks. You still got some of those little packets you made up?'

'Yep, in the back of the ute. Fuses are in the glove box; firing control on the front seat.' 'They take one of 'em out?'

'Maybe, but I wouldn't count on it. I'd chuck a grenade into the turret or smoke 'em out and let the machine guns take 'em down. You can try the urea, but you'd need a lot of it.'

Patch came out and joined the two men. 'Did the PM tell you I got the beast going?'

'Yep, but can you fly it? It's been what - twenty years from your last flight - and you nearly crashed then,' John said, remembering the flight on Devils.

'Ah, that! It was a stupid mistake. Those young girls on the beach were so hot I couldn't take my eyes off 'em.'

'Take it you've got your head around the controls?' 'Yep, ready to go. Why?'

'Well Patch, you fly tonight. Back-up for Richard's away team.'

'In this weather?'

'Yep. You're the gun pilot; you've flown in worse conditions than this. Remember Botswana?' John replied.

'Yeah, but I was current then, flying every day' Patch demurred, hesitant to fly the beast in the rain on his first solo.

'Walk in the park for a bloke of your skills' John said. 'Go get kitted up.' 'Need a co-pilot.'

John grinned. 'Bring the yank pilot out here.'

CHAPTER TWENTY-SEVEN

'So I take it you're not ready to die yet?' John asked the American captain, whose name tag was on his flight suit. Philips. 'You're the President's grandson, yes?'

"If I am?'

'A smart arse as well huh? Do you know who that other fella in there with you is?' 'Which one?'

'Pillman.'

Philips sat down, his hands still tied up. 'He's a good soldier. Takes orders without question.' 'He's a killer.' Richard countered. 'Do you know what you are really doing here?'

'Yes, flight time. Getting my hours up for a command posting.'

'You're dumber than I thought. You're out here, not in a real uniform, flying a killing machine that attacks civilian targets. Doesn't that seem a little strange to you?'

'I'm an American Marine pilot. I do what I'm told when I'm told.'

Richard walked over to him, grabbed his head and twisted. He pushed it back. 'Clean skin.'

'What's that all about?' Philips demanded.

'You're not the enemy, but you are working for the enemy.' 'Don't follow?'

'When you get back into the room with Pillman, check out the three small dots behind his left ear. Ask him what they're for and what his NWC are about to do.' John walked him back to the cell. 'Ask him.'

An hour later Max walked past the door. Philips called him over. 'Need to see Kelly and the other guy now.'

'Did he tell you?' John asked

'It's madness. You've just signed another recruit Major Kelly. I can't believe my grandfather is behind this.'

'Him and many other millionaires' son. They want total control of the world and will stop at nothing to get it. So you see we're just trying to save our own country. We mean no harm but will destroy our enemies come hell or high water. In Australia we have something called mateship. It's earned, not given. Take on one Aussie and you take us all on.'

'Well this Yank is not going to stand back and let this happen. Pillman said something about 2pm tomorrow.'

'H hour son, H hour' John said. 'I need you to prove yourself. Out behind those hills are tanks. You and Patch are going to go out there and put 'em out of action before our humble house is a pile of rocks. You up for that, maybe even killing some of your own countrymen?'

'If they are what you say they are they're no friends of mine. My dad told me as a kid, never let a bully get away with it. I fly with your man.'

'Your father's a wise man,' John declared, handing Philips a beer. Max removed his ties.

Indigo Base

The small commuter jet set down on the long runway. The pilot was amazed at the row of C130 aircraft and the line of helicopters. These were war machines; he had seen them on TV. He gunned his engines and was soon back in the air.

'What the fuck?' Brian said, placing the barrel of his pistol into the man's stomach. 'Turn around and put her down.'

'I land this fucker down there and there is no way I'll get off the ground again. You've got gunships and Herc's. I don't know what this is all about and I don't want to get mixed up in it.'

Brian reached over and opened the door. He unclipped the pilot's seat belt then fired the hand gun. He pushed the pilot out. Taking over the controls he returned to the base.

'Fuck, my five grand is still in his pocket.'

Taylor came out to welcome them. 'Your choppers are ready and they know where he is. I've got the tanks on the ground as back-up. You leave in ten.'

Brian nodded. 'It's all go then. You got a layout map?'

Taylor handed it to him. 'The building is partly destroyed from our last raid.'

'I want a night drop. Another hour,' Brian said. 'My boys are going to take a shower.'

Taylor walked back to the control room and sat down next to the man who would launch the missiles. 'Have you got them all back?'

'Sir, and locked our intruder out. Only way he can get into the system is when they fly, and he'd need an HF radio connected to his computer on a splitter device. Oh, and he'd also need to be at around ten thousand feet, or in direct line with a dish that I don't believe he has.'

'Good. Make sure those Tridents are first in the air.'

'Only have one back on line sir. The others are not accepting my commands.'

'Keep working on it. H hour is 1400. Order the ground crew to fuel the ICBM's and recheck the Tridents.'

Frazer's

The Apache lifted off. No lights were visible. Patch was disappointed he was not in the pilot's seat. The rain continued to belt down. Richard had his men depart. Leaving with the equipment, he hoped the Yank tank crew were on down time with the weather.

The chopper swung south, away from the hills where the tanks were.

'We're going to circle and come in behind,' Philips said, switching on the armaments computer. 'You ever used one of these?'

'No,' Patch replied.

'Okay. Your helmet is your master sights. All the weapons will follow your line of vision.

Select the ammo type stay, lock on and squeeze the little button on your stick. Simple as that.' Philips handed Patch the control stick for the armaments.

East of Frazer's Homestead

'Drop in five,' the pilot said. 'Better get back and do your checks.'

Brian walked back, holding up five fingers to his three-man team. They began their pre jump checks, then gave a thumbs up.

The rear door of the C130 began to open. Darkness greeted the line of men. It was still raining a little as Brian watched the jump light, waiting for it to turn green.

Green came on. The four men silently slipped into the darkness. Not a trace of them could be seen from the rear of the aircraft, which now banked away from the target and made tracks for the base at Indigo.

Philips, observing this activity in his radar scope, commented 'Aircraft in our area at ten thousand. He's dropped four packages.'

Patch looked at the small screen and saw four small dots appear. 'What do you make of it?' 'Parachutes are my guess. Better call your buddies and let them know to expect visitors.'

Patch took the radio, flicked it to the station channel and advised of four incoming by air drop. Richard soon had his men heading east. His night vision goggles scanned the land, reflecting a green image as he searched for hot spots. He stretched the men out to cover more territory. This type of work was what he was trained for. Hide and seek he called it. The idea was to find and not be found.

Ginger called in; he had spotted one of the chutes, about to land around three thousand ahead. 'Got a creek line here - make a good fire point.'

Richard and his team veered right and set up a typical frontal ambush; machine gun on the highest ground, AK 47's in close quarters to maximise fire power. The men lay in wait. Rain trickled down their faces. They were used to this type of living.

A branch snapped nearby. Richard honed in on the direction, scanning with his night vision.

It was a kangaroo going about its business. He relaxed a little, his finger still resting near the trigger guard. He flicked the safety off. He knew the roo was a dead giveaway.

More noises came from his left. Once again he scanned. This time it was a mob of roos in a hurry. He spoke quietly into his field comms. 'Left eleven o'clock, range five hundred. I see two.'

Richard heard the fifty being cocked and the safeties of the other AK's being clicked off. The boys were ready. He waited, wondering how many more were coming and, more to the point, where they were. He gave the order.

'Flick to night-sites. Pick own targets.'

The Fifty clattered, sending four balls and one trace toward the three men. They hit the deck and were soon returning fire. Brian locked onto the barrel flashes and aimed, controlling his breathing. He squeezed his trigger. He heard the thump of the rounds hitting rocks or timber. He waited again for return fire.

Three bursts of small arms fire came at him. He ducked down into the creek as the bullets zinged overhead. The Fifty cracked again; this time it found a target. He heard the man scream, then the whole area became silent. A trick Richard knew well. Their enemies had embarked on a flanking move. He warned his men. They lay in position for another fifteen minutes; it was still quiet except for the sound of rain falling. He flicked his comms on.

'They've bugged out.'

Richard went to the area where he had heard the man scream, and found him propped against a tree with no less than five hits in his body. He had used himself as an attractor so the others could bug out. Not an uncommon trick. He had seen it used many times in Iraq. Draw the fire and give your buddies a fair escape route. Normally done by a wounded bloke who knew his number was up.

'We fell for one of the oldest tricks in the book' he thought.

Richard returned to his men. 'Come on, we've gotta get back to the homestead before they do. Can't use the bikes, they'll make us a target. We've gotta hump it.'

They set off at a pounding pace toward the homestead.

The Chopper

It swung in low. Philips kept it beneath the tree line and switched on the forward scanner. 'We've got six tanks.'

'Can this machine take em all?' Patch asked.

'They're Abrahams. Toughest bastard of a tank known. If you're gonna take 'em on it has to be from the rear. That's the thinnest armour.'

He hovered the chopper. The tank troop leader heard the thump of the rotors and waved, thinking it was from the base.

'They think we're theirs,' Philips said. 'They're going to get a bit of a shock. You ready with the rockets?'

Patch nodded.

'Your helmet sight will identify four at a time, then pick the best shot for you. Just keep the cross-hairs on the target. Once hit it will automatically select the second, and so on. I'll run us down that narrow passage.'

Philips dipped the front of the chopper forward and applied full power. The beast lurched forward. Patch had targets in his sights, and saw small numbers come up on his hood. He took the fire stick, selected the side winders and pushed the button. The first tank was hit in the rear and was soon in flames. He must have found the gas tank. The crews on the ground ran to their tanks and the turrets were soon pointed at the chopper.

Philips lowered the aircraft, skimming over the ground, skids swiping small trees. Patch fired again, but the front of the turret took the hit. Nothing seemed to happen. He selected Manual Target Acquire, fixed the cross hairs onto the rear portion and fired. Once again, flames flew from the rear of the tank. The crew began to bail out. Patch flicked to cannon and squeezed the fire button. The earth in front boiled with bullets hitting the ground and what remained of the tank. He sprayed the side of the tank, taking out the escaping men.

The chopper shuddered as a mass of machine gun fire from one of the tanks strafed its side. Patch felt one bullet go deep into his chest. He slumped forward, pushing hard on the control. Blood from his chest sprayed over the instrument panel.

Philips tried to recover the chopper as it went into a spin just five feet from the ground. It exploded into flames as it smashed into the ground at over a hundred knots. The flames soon engulfed the aluminium frame and burned bright orange. Then the remaining ordnance exploded, sending a wall of flame into the air.

CHAPTER TWENTY-EIGHT

Richard's Away Team

Lightning lit the night sky, illumining the earth. An old stone station hut used by cattle-hands came into view. Richard noticed a small light coming from the building. Stopping his men, he signalled for a frontal attack. He had the Fifty set up.

'Give us five, then open fire,' he instructed the machine gun operator.

The remainder of the team moved forward in a tactical line. Richard checked his watch. One minute till all hell would break loose. He was now only fifty yards from the stone building. He could hear voices inside.

'This is not the fucking homestead,' one yelled. 'It's an outstation!'

Richard smirked. 'Okay, hit the deck!,' he screamed. The Fifty chattered and sustained its rate of fire for a good minute Richard could see the trace flying overhead then slamming into the building. The occupants returned fire but the cover of darkness didn't give them a clear target. He looked behind and could see the muzzle flashes of the Fifty as it continued its barrage of fire.

The building began to crumble from the onslaught of fire. Rocks that had stood for one hundred years gave way. It eventually collapsed exposing the inside.

Another flash of lightning showed Richard three very scared men huddled in the rocks.

'Drop them and you live, fire and you die right here,' he yelled.

Gunfire came from the building, which Richard returned. He didn't hold back, his finger hard on the trigger as he sprayed the pile of rock. The rest of his team joined in. The Fifty began to fire again. Soon the building fell silent. Richard called a stop and inched forward. He found two bodies. Amazingly, one had escaped the onslaught.

Frazer's

Rain continued to fall. Large puddles had now formed on the hard red soil at the front of the house.

'Where are Richard and the boys?' John asked Jillian. 'Not sure. Didn't he go after the tanks or something?'

'Well as soon as he gets back, tell him to go to his fire point. We have to try and stop them now.'

'Where are you going?' Jillian asked. 'Same, to my position.'

'I don't want to stay here by myself,' she pleaded, panic stricken.

John walked toward the puddles on the ground. He knew the black sinking soil would have the tanks stuck fast. Currently they posed no threat. He turned back to her.

'I need you to be strong here Jillian. I'll have a man stay with you. Doc will be here too.' 'I thought Doc was going with you to run your medical post?'

'He won't be needed till the shooting starts. Then he'll fly to the evac position near the cattle yards. Max and Rat will stay. They're good men.'

'You take care John. I want you back in one piece. Both of us do' she said, rubbing her tummy.

One Day Later Canberra ACT- 0700 local time.

Grey called the meeting to order. Only those who were part of the NWC were present. He rose from his seat and cleared his throat.

'Now is the time to get your families out. D-day is 2pm tomorrow. Tasmania's not on the strike list so that's the safest place to go.'

'What about our closest friends?' someone at the back of the room asked.

'When we agreed to this, friends were not included, only close family. We are about to become the new commanders of this planet. We can't afford hangers-on. It's going to be a long and difficult road. We don't need the pain of fostering friends and others simply because we don't want to see them die. On the table are your tickets for wives and families. The planes leave in two hours. I suggest you be on them.'

Mike Taylor returned to the launch room, and addressed Trident Missile control. 'They ready?'

'Got two back. The other three will drop right back on top of us,' the controller said.

'The President wants an early launch of these Tridents. He has a fleet off the coast ready to come in and take over. What cities have we got online?'

'Sydney and Melbourne, the two most populated.' 'Change Melbourne to Canberra, can you do that?' 'Yes Sir I can. It will take me a couple of minutes.' 'Call me when you're done.'

'Sir - Canberra, that's where our top people in Australia are.'

'Not for much longer. America wants it all.' Grey got up. 'Remember, call me soon as they are online.'

John climbed up to where he had hidden the firing gear. He rechecked everything. The rainstorm had not done much damage, but he was unsure about the explosives buried deep in the rock face. He did not have the time to check. Suddenly he heard a hissing sound, then saw tail fire as two of the trident missiles were launched heavenward.

John stared in disbelief as the missiles began to arch towards the east. He heard the chatter of the Fifty followed by the RPG's slamming into the remaining tridents. They fell to the ground.

Gas began to leak out of the delivery heads, drifting along the ground. The breeze began to shepherd it towards the buildings in the complex.

The cattle came thundering down the valley into the canyon. As predicted, the NWC security force were scrambling to escape, some falling to the ground holding their throats as the gas took effect.

Those who made it out of the danger zone were now following the cows as the movement sensors went off one at a time. Sirens at the camp screamed. When the security forces reached the ambush point, John slammed the plunger down. The rocky sides of the canyon collapsed, blocking their retreat to the base.

Roo moved forward. 'Take out the generators.'

Fletch aimed one of the RPG's, fired it and soon the power house was in flames.

On his return, Roo took control of the Fifty, aimed it and was about to push down on the fire lever, when bullets began to thud around him. Taking flight, he yelled to his men

"Pull back!"

Frazer's

Dicko watched as the tall ICBM climbed skywards.

'Hey Doc, crank up your plane, we got work to do!' he yelled, gathering his laptop and locations book.

Jillian came running. 'Doc's not here! He flew out to the cattle yards.'

Dicko ran out to the satellite dish, connected his computer, then called for Jillian. She arrived, wondering what all the panic was about.

'When I tell you, move the dish and follow that rocket.' He tapped on the key pad.

'God, I hope this works.'

The other four ICBM's headed skywards. 'Fuck!' he shouted. 'On my mark, track them.' Jillian gripped the dish with both hands.

'Now!' he shouted.

Jillian followed the missiles as Dicko entered data. He picked up the change code, removed old coordinates and replaced them with new ones.

'Here goes!' he muttered, hitting Enter.

A few seconds later, the missiles changed direction and headed North East. Dicko grabbed Jillian and began to dance around.

'We did it Prime Minister, we did it!'

'Did what?' Jillian asked with great excitement

'Return to sender! Boomeranged 'em back to the sickos who made 'em.'

Happy at what he had achieved, Dicko settled down and glanced at the news page. His jaw dropped.

'Dear God, they've wiped out most of Canberra and half of Sydney.' Jillian stopped walking, and turned.

'What are you saying?'

'Shit!' Dicko exclaimed, handing her the laptop.

Jillian dropped the computer, fell to her knees and burst into tears. Canberra. Their son was still at the Academy. Her secretary and housekeeper, loyal, average people who kept the nation running, now dead. Sydney! She had a lot of friends who lived there too, people with young families. Gone. All gone. She sobbed and sobbed as Dicko tried to console her. 'Who did this Dicko? Who?'

He hugged her. 'Jillian, it was the greedy and corrupt power mongers of America. They want the whole country.'

'I damn well hope that's where you returned those missiles to.' He pulled her closer, not sure what to say.

Indigo Base

Corpses littered the compound, dead from the nerve agent. Roo kept his men at a safe distance from the noxious vapours still moving along the ground.

'Let's go home,' he said, turning his back on the destruction he had helped create.

CHAPTER TWENTY-NINE

'We have five incoming Sir, just past Hawaii! Estimate mainland impact in twenty minutes!

Targeting Washington, New York, Dallas, Chicago and Newport.'

'Scramble all interceptors! Blow the fuckers out of the sky before one drop of that shit reaches mainland America!' General Marks yelled. 'And get me the President on the phone – now!'

The Console Operator Sergeant spun around in his chair.

'Have scrambled out of Hawaii and all bases on the west coast. President on line one.' 'Updates every two minutes!' the General screamed. Into the phone he said

'No Mister President, they're from the Indigo project. The delivery address was sabotaged.'

'Enable Self-destruct – now!'

'Sorry Sir, it's been disabled. We're unable to access the on-board computers to make it work.'

The anxiety in the President's voice was palpable.

'Tony, we can't let them get through. Millions of Americans will die.'

I'm aware of that Sir. Airforce is tracking them and two fighters closing in within missile range.'

'Targets?' The president asked.

'Airforce one being prepped now Sir. Your chopper collects you in three.' 'I asked for fucking targets!'

General Marks gave him the targets, then hung up and turned to the room. 'You've got ten minutes to ring your families and say goodbye.'

'Sir! One down! The other pilot has a lock on number two and the west coasters are closing in on the other three.'

'Put a hold on those calls, people. We just might nail this'

'Three down sir, two still inbound, lost in cloud cover. A fighter has gone after them.' Marks glanced at the clock. Six minutes.

'Four Sir, the other has got away. It's heading for New York.'

Canberra. 16 July 2015. 3pm

The streets that were normally bustling with traffic were deserted. Cars were piled up; hundreds dead on the streets.

Entire buildings that had sucked the gas in through air conditioners were silent, including the airport. The Federal Government of Australia was no more, all dignitaries asphyxiated by deadly gas. Employees had dropped in the corridors. Nothing that breathed air survived as the gas- clouds drifted over the suburbs.

Woden Shopping Centre, one of Canberra's largest, resembled Pompeii after the volcano. Trolleys of groceries stood abandoned. Mothers, babies and teenagers lay dead on the ground. Russell Office, base of the country's top military personnel, had fared no better.

News reports of varying accuracy began to flood the media across the remainder of the country. State premiers seized this opportunity to graduate to the big league, promising a stable government to replace obliterated leaders, and jockeying for their city to be the new political capital, Melbourne flexing its muscle as the most densely populated.

The extent of personal loss made citizens indifferent to internal political debate. People banded together to help search for missing friend and relatives, though the unknown nature of the attack saw them turned away by what remained of the Defence Force, now mobilised from remaining cities. They had declared the besieged cities unsafe to enter.

Banks closed ATM's had locked customers out, as did thousands of shopping centres for fear of further attacks. Public transport ground to a halt along with domestic and international flights. The country was in lockdown. Remaining civilian police struggled to maintain law and order.

Frazer's

John ran in, threw down his pack and stood stunned. Jillian, her face disfigured from crying, hurried to meet him.

'Have you heard?'

'It's all over the radio. The bastard never intended a 1400 hour strike. They brought it forward Jillian! I have contributed to the destruction of thousands if not millions of my own countrymen.'

She hugged him strongly.

'It's not your fault darling. You acted with integrity on the information you had at hand.' John buried his head in his hands, shaking it slowly in disbelief.

'Our son was in Canberra John.'

'I know, and I am so sorry I didn't stop them. I killed our boy, the son I didn't even get to meet.'

John broke down and wept on Jillian's shoulder. Through tears he blurted out

'I was trained to stop exactly this from happening! To serve and protect my nation, to die trying.'

Jillian enfolded him in her arms and kissed him.

'You've had such a hard life John. So have your men. You weren't to know what these people were capable of. Dicko managed to turn the ICBM's back to the States. I know that's no consolation, but it was one of your ideas from the start.'

Washington

The rocket deployed its ten heads. Each contained a small GPS which targeted the suburbs. The main rocket exploded sending the nerve gas into the air. Seconds later, as the smaller heads found their destinations, they did the same. Poisonous clouds drifted towards the ground, destroying air-breathing life as they descended. Three million people now were in its path as it engulfed the city.

The President never made it from the Whitehouse to his Air Force One helicopter. The NWC centre occupants on 5th Avenue met the same fate.

Frazer's

A hundred metres away, Brian, from the American crack Seal team was the only who'd eluded John's men, sat on a hill overlooking the old homestead. The once stately building was now a pile of rocks. His field binoculars focussed on people in the shed nearby; a woman conversing with a man. He recognised her.

'Bonus!' he murmured menacingly.

Jillian had been pacing back and forth, trying to decide where her duty lay.

'I need to return to Canberra. I have to make some kind of parliament out of this mess!'

'You can't at the moment' John countered. 'That gas is active for 72 hours. Then we'll both go. I want the nation to know what really happened, and to give our son his final farewell, one he deserves' John said, choking up again.

Brian noticed the woman moving desolately toward the small building at the side of the shed. He leered and was behind the outside toilet before she got there. This was an opportunity not to be missed. He waited – she'd be out soon.

Jillian finished what she had to do, stepped out and turned to close the door. She felt a hand go over her mouth. Strong arms lifted her sixty kilo body like a rag doll. Though struggling, she was borne away in silence.

When they reached the pump-shed on the other side of the ridge, Brain shoved her inside and flicked the chain over to the latch, checking that Jillian would not be able to kick the door open.

'Where is Captain Philips?' he asked, sitting in front of the door.

'I don't know. He went away and hasn't returned. Who are you? What do you want?' Jillian shouted across the noise of the pump-shed.

'My mission is to safely return the President's grandson. You don't need to know any more than that.'

'Do you know what your country has just done? They've bombed Canberra and Sydney with nerve gas, killed millions of people, including my only son. So fuck you!' she shouted.

'Can if you like honey, don't mind the women on top,' he replied, laughing at his captive. John's nerves were shredded by the dramatic turn of events. All his senses were on high alert.

Noticing Jillian's protracted absence, he asked 'Has anyone seen Jillian?'

'She's in the ladies,' Bardi replied. 'Missing her already?' 'Shut it Bardi!' John snapped.

Bardi shrugged at the rebuff, but rose and sauntered outside toward the toilet, noticing boot prints in the mud at the rear of the small building. American army boots. He could tell by the imprint that the wearer was carrying weight.

'Boss!' he yelled 'We've got a problem – she's gone, carried away.' He pointed to the prints on the ground. 'They went that way.'

Now gagged and tied, Jillian tried to resist the man dragging her along the rough terrain with his toggle rope. He pulled harder as they started up the incline to the small cave which had been his hideout for the past 48 hours. Small bushes ripped at her shirt, exposing her to his lewd gaze.

'Don't worry darling, I'll be seeing much more than your tits.' He laughed again. 'I'm going to enjoy fucking the answer out of you.'

He pushed Jillian into the cave, which was concealed by bushes and overhanging rocks, and tied her to a tree trunk that had penetrated a crack in the rock face. He checked her hand ties.

Happy they were secured, he stepped back to look at her exposed breast. There was nothing Jillian could do to cover herself. She turned her head away.

'Take it a babe like you has a lover back at that shed?' Jillian remained silent.

'My guess is you have, I think it was that guy you were talking to before nature called. I reckon that dude is John Kelly.'

'Well if it is, he is going to kick your arse all over this cattle station,' Jillian replied, desperately hoping John had noticed her absence and was looking for her.

'Real tough man, ha?' Brian asked.

'Tough! You wouldn't know the meaning of the word. Your kind needs hundreds of troops behind you before you'll do anything.'

Brain strode over and slapped her face.

'I am a Seal lady, a fucking Seal! The best soldiers in the world.' Blood trickled from the corner of Jillian's mouth.

'A woman beater is all you are. Real tough mister. More like a seal puppy.'

'A funny bitch eh?'

He struck out again, this time with a clenched fist to the side of her face. He ripped what remained of her blouse from her, and fondled her breast.

'Man, am I going to enjoy you lady. Boy, am I!' 'Dish it out but can't take it huh, tough guy?'

Fearing his next blow might finish his intended prey, Brian walked outside to cool down a little. He needed food. That would mean leaving Jillian in the cave. She was secure; that was not the problem. The men at the shed; by now they'd know she was missing. The natives in Australia were as astute as his Arapahoe ancestors at tracking.

Taking his rifle, Brian picked up his tracks at the bottom of the hill and made others to create confusion. He headed off in a totally different direction towards a windmill where he had seen kangaroos. The water trough was an ideal place to shoot one.

Further down the gully, Bardi was moving slowly, scanning for signs of disturbed ground; a broken twig or stones dislodged by footprints.

Bardi set off again like a greyhound on a rabbit trail.

John followed, in envious appreciation of his colleague's bush skills.

A rifle shot sounded. Bardie looked skyward, then pointed. 'This way. Those birds have given him away.'

Both men broke into a run. It was not long before they saw their quarry. He was busy butchering what remained of a small kangaroo.

John broke left as Bardi headed right, and they silently advanced upon Jillian's abductor. Famished, their quarry was absorbed in the task at hand. John grabbed him, spun him around and swung a punch which connected with Brain's shoulder. The Seal landed on the ground.

'That your best shot, tough man?' he barked at John.

He got to his feet with his knife, bloodied from the roo, gripped firmly in his hand. He swung out at John, who jumped back as the weapon came close to his gut. He kicked out but Brian swung the knife again, this time slicing John's leg.

'Come on Aussie, you can do better than that.'

John fell to the ground, his leg bleeding. His hand found a tree-branch. He swung it but it was rotten with white ants and shattered into pieces as it struck its target.

Brian came in for the killer blow. Knife high in the air, his shadow fell over John lying on the ground. Bardi fired his rifle. Brian stopped mid-stride, suddenly realizing his predicament. He dropped the knife and put his hands up.

'Took two of you fuckers.'

'Where's the girl?' John demanded.

'Girl? What girl?' Brian replied, realising Jillian was his life insurance. If he gave her up, he figured he'd be dead meat.

Bardi pushed his rifle into Brian's back.

'Walk, arsehole! I know how to make you talk, Seal-meat.'

John hastily tied a field dressing onto his leg, then hobbled after Bardi and the Seal.

CHAPTER THIRTY

Frazer's shed. Ants and Gum-Tree Goo

Doc tended to John's leg, insisting on a few stitches, though the cut was not deep. 'Sick of patching this war horse up,' he joked, administering a shot of local anaesthetic.

Bardi and his Aboriginal friends were holding Brian captive outside. 'Hey Charlie, go and get some of the blood from the tall trees.'

Bardi looked around until he found a meat-ants' nest. He muttered to his men in their dialect, and soon they had made a rack over the Ants nest. Charlie returned with a lump of red sap he had extracted from the tree, and handed it to Bardi, who said

'Bring the yank here.'

They sat Brian down on the ground and explained the fate awaiting him.

'See this, fella? ants can't resist the red sap – they swarm over it like bees on a honey pot.'

Bardi picked off some of the sticky gum-sap and smeared it on the ground, which very soon moved like water as the ants swarmed to devour it.

'See what I mean?'

Brian watched in trepidation as the ants rapidly consumed the goo, then carried what was left back to their nests. Charlie and the others grabbed him and lay him on the rack stark naked, tying him into place with leg and wrist ropes. Bardi spread the red goo over his testicles and along his leg, then down the wooden leg of the rack towards the ants' nest.

'Tell me where she is and I'll kick the trail away.' Brian said nothing.

The ground once again boiled with millions of meat ants pouring out of their nest towards the red sap. It didn't take long for the insects to find the trail to the rack leg and on his body. Within a few minutes Brian's testicles were a metropolis of meat-ants. They bit his soft skin and drew blood, signalling a kill. More ants joined the frenzy.

Brian began to scream as he felt his genitals being ripped from his body.

Bardi took out his knife and made small cuts all over his body. Detecting more blood, the ants swarmed to the cuts, Brain tried to buck to be rid of the insects.

'Get them off! I'll tell you!' he shouted.

Charlie took a leaf-switch and began to slap the ants away. Brain's balls were grotesquely swollen; he had welts all over his body from the bites. Bardi leant over him, his face inches away.

'Where is she?'

Brian spat at Bardi. 'Fuck off, nigger.'

Bardi stood up.

'Your party bro. We'll recall the ants and flies; back soon. See ya when the maggots are crawling out of those cuts. Charlie, billy time.'

Leaving Brian to a second Ant-siege, plus the blow flies that had landed on his open cuts, the men walked away to sit in the shade of a tree while the billy boiled. They jabbered away in their native tongue, taking bets on Brian's pain threshold. Ten minutes was the longest wager.

In the Cave

Jillian froze, hardly daring to breathe. A large spinifex snake had slithered into the cool of the cave. As its yellow-tinged body flowed over the rocks near her, she figured it was at least seven feet long. It curled into a circle, head resting on its body, forked tongue testing the air, then struck suddenly at a Rat that appeared from a crack in the rocks. It went into convulsions as the snake's venom attacked its tiny body. Jillian tried to stay stock still, fearing the snake would make her its next meal.

To compound her horror, a very large bird spider soon crawled down the rock face and headed in her direction. She was not sure what she feared most, the spider or the snake which was now consuming its kill. The spider came closer. She could see its pincers as it traversed over the rock. She wanted to scream but the gag muffled her noises.

Surrender

Brian screamed louder as freshly-laid juvenile maggots burrowed into his flesh. The ants had returned and were also feasting on him again. Bardi approached, looked resolutely down at him, and again asked.

'Where?'

'A cave just over the ridge, near the old pump shed.'

Charlie was soon running up the hill towards the cave. He burst inside and saw the snake vanish through a cleft as it sensed approaching danger. He slapped his hand on the spider, crushing its body against the rocks. Its guts oozed through his fingers.

'You okay Missus?'

Jillian was soon untied, her gag removed. 'Just get me out of here, please.'

She flung her arms around Charlie's neck as he helped her outside into the sunlight. 'We got the fella that took you lady - we make 'im talk.'

Jillian's knees buckled from all the recent shock. Charlie picked her up to carry her back to the shed, then stopped, took off his shirt and covered Jillian.

'Not good them fella's see ya like this.'

He picked her up again and smiled warmly down at her. She felt safe in his arms as he carried her back. John hobbled out of the shed. Seeing Jillian's limp form, he feared the worst.

'She a-okay boss,' Charlie said reassuringly, passing her over to him.

Doc came to the door.

'Don't you rip those bloody stitches out Kelly. I haven't got any more.' He then hurried over to examine Jillian.

'Get her inside. She's in shock.'

Bardi released Brian, a few ants still feasting on his body.

'Walk! Don't stop. If bossman see you again, he kill ya.'

Barefoot and naked, Brian ran off towards the bush, putting maximum space between him and the natives. Charlie came over.

'I win! Ten bucks. How long you bet on him this time?'

'Two days Charlie. Double or nothing.' Bardi grinned.

Charlie shook hands with Bardi.

'You forget. He's 'eadin' for Death Adder Valley. I give him maybe till tonight.'

John hung over Doc as he treated Jillian.

'If you don't get your ugly moosh outa my way I'll stitch it shut. Move out of my light, dingo- breath!'

Richard came over and dragged John away. 'How long is that airstrip?'

'Why?'

'Me and the boys wanna get a plane out of here. To help clean up Canberra. Your boys and the PM are welcome to come with us.'

'Yep, it's about time I stopped running. The airstrip's fifteen hundred metres; you'll get a Herc on it no problem.'

'I'll make the call.' Richard walked over to Dicko.

'Get me the nearest Australian Air Force base. We need a lift out of here.'

CHAPTER THIRTY-ONE

Canberra. Four Days after the Attack

As the Australian C130 aircraft settled onto the runway at Canberra airport, those who had been evacuated from Frazer's were confronted with the stark aftermath of the nerve-gas bombing. Lines of six C130's were parked in many rows, as numerous military personnel stacked pallets of body bags onto trucks to be loaded onto waiting aircraft. Jillian stood on the steps of the plane, weeping silently at the macabre spectacle unfolding before her. An airforce staff car stopped near the C130. The driver did a double-take, realising his passenger was in truth the nation's missing Prime Minister.

John walked her to the car, then stopped and spoke to Richard the former SAS leader 'What now?'

'Go over to one of those pup officers; tell him who we are and that we're here to help put this city back together.'

John shook his hand.

'Tell your men from me - thanks. I'll have the PM get your money to you.' He smiled. 'Been a pleasure to serve with you. Captain - I believe?'

'What about you?' Richard enquired.

'I've got a few things to do here, then I plan to build my Utopia back at Frazer's. You and your boys are more than welcome anytime you're in the area.'

'Well, best of luck Major. You're one hell of a task master, and tell that Roo he cuts a mean training course!'

Kelly's men stood in line near the aircraft and shook hands with Richard as he passed. John asked the driver if he could organise a truck for some very tired soldiers, and take them to the accommodation block in town.

The Premier of Victoria walked over and leaned through the window of the staff car. Addressing Jillian, he said

'So - the rat returns.'

John sprang from the car, shirt-fronted the Premier and pushed him against the vehicle. 'The rat - as you put it mister - saved the rest of our capital cities from the same fate as this place. What were you doing to stop it? Speak to her like that again and I'll cut your balls out and make you eat them. Savvy?'

John released him and noticed urine trickling down his leg.

'Pretty fucking tough when you have backers, you piece of shit.' John said as he walked back to the car and got in.

'Let's hit the road.'

'Where to Ma'am?' enquired the driver. 'Home first. I need a long shower.'

'You are probably not aware ma'am, but the Victorian Premier has moved into the Lodge.' 'Well, he has a surprise coming, hasn't he?'

As the vehicle exited the compound, the military continued to pack hundreds of body bags onto trucks. She felt sick imagining how they died, and for what?

'How many dead, do you know driver?'

'Not sure Ma'am; I've heard around the 120,000 mark.' 'My God! That's close to 80 percent.'

'Yep. They say Sydney's not much better.' 'The Royal Military College -did that get hit?'

'Yep, though most of the under-officers were on a course at Puckapunyal. They've been commandeered to take control at Russell and Campbell. The missile took out the whole nine yards; tax office and most other government departments. What a mess!'

'What's left of the government?'

'You're it I believe. Seems they tried to get out before the attack, but got caught right in the middle of it.'

He turned the staff car into the drive of the Lodge, and the shit hit the fan as she walked in. The premier was sitting drinking whiskey like he owned the place. He got up as they walked in.

'Can I help you?' he asked, somewhat pompously.

'Well, for starters you can nicky-boo out of my wee hut here, and secondly, you might like to replace that whisky. It's an expensive drop.'

The man's wife promptly left the room.

'I have to advise you that the Governor General appointed me as caretaker PM' he grinned. 'Thank you Mr Caretaker, but your residency terminates as of - now. My driver will help with your bags.'

He left the room. John looked at her. 'Remind me never to get on your bad side.'

The rest of the team were put up at a government hostel in the CBD. It was full of military helpers and civilian police who had been brought in. Roo walked around the dinner room, recognising a few old mates he had served with. Most of them thought he was still listed MIA. 'Nope – still here! Not dead or missing.'

'Who are the other blokes with you?' one asked. 'What's left of Delta Team.'

You still in, or out?' they asked.

'Civilian, my friends. Got dumped 20 years back. You blokes know where a fella can get a few drinks around here?'

'Only the Sergeants mess out at Royal Military College. Bring the boys; we'll sign you all in.'

'Ha! That's the best thing I've heard of in ages. Snake Pit eh? Haven't been in one for years.' Roo returned to his men and gave them the news.

'Boys, dress up a little will you?'

John walked around the Lodge. He had never been is such a stately place. He saw the photos of past Prime Ministers Hawke, Keating, Howard, and Jillian's father hung proudly on the walls, and remembered them all. He was a new, young officer when Hawke was in power. Those were the days he thought; young and stupid.

Jillian put the phone down and ran to John in tears of joy.

"He's alive John! Our son is alive! He was away when this happened. The Commandant of RMC is going to have him brought out here tonight.' she hugged John.

'Stone the crows! I'd better fire up the BBQ! You make a salad. We've got to feed a hungry army man.'

John felt chuffed but nervous. He was going to meet his son.

He drank a beer as he warmed the hotplate, noticing his hand shaking as he put the bottle to his mouth. To take his mind off things, he whistled an old tune, "Rebel Blood In my Veins."

A car pulled into the drive. Jillian was in the bedroom getting changed. John saw the lights swing past. He wiped his hands, took a deep breath and strode to the door, unsure of his reception. When he opened it, a tall

young man stood before him wearing an officer's
uniform. John put his hand out.

'You must be John Gillman. I'm John Kelly.' The
boys started to buckle at the knees.

'I know who you are; my Gran eventually came clean
and told me everything, Dad.' Kelly burst into a smile
hearing the name he had wanted to hear for so long.

'Welcome home son.'

He pulled the boy towards him and held him, kissing
his cheeks and forehead. 'Hope you're hungry John, I've
got the barby on.'

Young John stepped inside. 'Mum about?'

John pointed. 'Shower.'

Kelly went to the fridge and brought back two beers.
He handed one to his son. 'So how long before
graduation?'

'Well, after the attack we were fast-tracked to
graduate early - to replace dead and missing officers. So
I take up my first appointment in a couple of weeks.'

He pointed to the gold pips on his shoulders.

'Well done! Who with?'

He looked at his father, then lowered his eyes. He
cleared his throat, met John's gaze and smiled.

'Special Ops, Strike Force Delta. I'll be the 2IC if I pass the induction.' 'Delta huh? Good mob them. You've done well.'

'Dad, I know it's your old unit. I want to do it proud, get it back to what it was when you were in command. What they did to you and your unit sucked, and our country's demise is the end result. I have to live with the shame that my own grandfather was the driving force behind it. He ripped us both off – all this time. I'm so sorry dad - what can I say?'

'No need for you to apologize son. You weren't even born when all that was done and dusted.'

'No but it denied us a family life. It chewed me up trying to figure out who my Dad was; what he did. Was he a good bloke or a drop-out? Two months ago Nanna sat me down and told me the whole story. That's why when Delta came up I jumped at the chance. Dad, a lot of the older officers admire you still. They're going to teach the "Devils Rock Incident" at the Academy, to make sure no one is ever caught in that situation again.'

John's son had tears forming in the corners of his eyes. 'Well, sounds like some good has come out of it after all.' 'You're not mad about it?'

Mad? Son, I am bitterly mad about what happened. Not only to me, but to my men. That hurts worst of all. Some of those men were married with young children. Like you, they were denied their father. That's what makes me maddest.'

'So what now?' young John asked.

'Clear your mother's name and reputation.' Jillian came out and ran to her son. They hugged. 'How are you Mum?'

He stood back and noticed her little baby bump. 'Are you, um, Preg.?'

Jillian stopped him.

'Yes son, eight weeks actually. You share a father!'

'Oh my God! I'm going to have a brother or sister! This is awesome!' He sounded so happy.

'Congratulations guys!'

'Come on John junior! You can show me what kind of cook you are,' Kelly said, walking towards the patio and taking another beer with him. When he was out of sight he jumped for joy.

His son was a man and a good man. He was going into Delta; that was the icing on the cake.

With his chest proudly out, he marched to the barby and tested the heat on the hotplate.

Next Morning

The city was continually busy. The stench of decaying bodies was overpowering. Flies were the most persistent pest. A special team was patrolling with insect spray to try and halt the spread of disease. Young John and his team of soldiers were in the thick of it.

An angry crowd waited at Parliament house. Press from all over the world were there. The Victorian Premier was nowhere to be seen. Jillian stepped from her C1 Commonwealth car. John alighted to the chant of people shouting 'Hang the bitch!'

Jillian walked tall and stopped at the podium. John nudged her out of the way, turned on the microphone and began his address.

"Most of you don't know who I am. I was the commander of an elite force known as Strike Team Delta. We were deployed by a former government on a mission some of may be aware of – the Devils Rock incident. A mission we undertook as soldiers who trust their democratic Government has integrity. However, to protect their corrupt ulterior motives, this particular government had you believe we were either Killed in Action or Missing in Action. We had our identities stripped away and were contained in a remote military prison to prevent us telling the truth. Well, as you can see we are neither dead nor missing.'

Gripping either side of the wooden podium, John continued.

"Before you pass judgement, I want you to hear what I have to say about our current PM. She is the mother of my son. She was denied having me around to be a father to him and a husband to her because her father didn't want his secret revealed. The secret of his involvement with a bunch of rich criminals called the New World Command. This organisation is subsidised by many wealthy power-brokers from all over the world, and leading American government officials.

Their under-the-table funding paid for big ticket campaigns to keep them in power. It also protected the deal they made with the Indigo land lease.

Indigo is in a very remote part of Australia, thus out of sight of the press. It was used to develop the takeover of the Middle East and destroy all Australian capital cities. America was going to become the dominant world power. With ownership of our resources they could set the price to the remainder of the world. Why? Greed and the need to feed their own population - at inflated prices.

Your Prime Minister, Jillian Gillman, discovered their plot. She asked me and my ex- Delta team if we could help her. We did, but too late to stop some of the missiles. The Prime Minister was out there with us, taking on the NWC to try to prevent what happened.

When we arrived today, I heard some of you wanted to hang her. For what? Giving a damn about her country and the people she leads? Besides a group of discontented former Desert Storm soldiers we didn't see any of you people out helping. Why? Because it was kept from you by the very Ministers serving under this woman. This was in return for early warning of the pending attack so they could get to safety and leave you people behind. Bit gutless I figure. But please listen to what Jillian has to say to you before you tie that rope around a tree branch. Thank you.'

John stepped back from the podium.

Jillian steps up.

'Thank you John, and my condolences to all people who are even now experiencing such grief and loss. I have contacted the Governor General, and as there are no elected people left to run the country, we both agree that I step down as PM. A group of well qualified people have been approached to step in until full elections can be conducted. Given it was a party that did this to the country, I urge you all to vote for independents who will represent the people, and not a party line. A full release of this tragedy and its perpetrators will be made available to the media, including the naming and shaming of those who financially backed the New World Council for their own gains. No more secrets ladies and gentlemen. It stops now. Thank you and may God bless you all.'

Jillian stepped back. To reporters shoving microphones under her nose and firing questions at her wanting to know more, she said pleasingly

'Wait for the release documents.'

As they climbed into the waiting C1 vehicle, Roo and the men applauded. John asked 'What about you fellas?'

'Getting our lives back in order. Married guys who still have families heading home. You still hellbent on creating your Utopia?'

'Yep.'

'Maybe see you there, at Frazer's' Roo said, saluting John.

'Tell Richard and his boys, they are welcome as well.
There's room enough for us all. You're family to us
now.'

CHAPTER THIRTY-TWO

Six Months Later

Doc and Roo sat back and admired the new house at the waterhole. 'Think they'll like it?' Doc asked.

'Well it's where he wanted to build. It's quiet, has running water and is far enough away from the rest of the community. Come on mate, we got to make sure your surgery's moving along. Richard and his merry men are waiting down at the flats for their kit homes to arrive, so it's about time you made that call to John.

Doc stopped the ute near the gates to Frazer's, took out the sign and yelled to Roo 'C'arn ya big bugger, give us a hand to put this thing up will ya?'

Canberra

Elections were over. The people had spoken and elected a new party to govern. It seemed party driven politics would forever dictate their needs and wishes.

John walked into the PM's office.

'So, what now?' he asked.

Jillian now well and truly showing and glowing, picked up her handbag and flicked off the computer.

'Dunno about you, but I've got an appointment with Doc at Utopia. Coming?

John grinned, indicating the grandeur of their surroundings with a sweeping gesture. 'And all of this, milady?'

'I have done my time John. I'm not one to look back.'

Several days later, as their family wagon pulled into Frazer's driveway, they saw a sign high above the front gate.

"Welcome to Utopia."

THE END

www.ingramcontent.com/pod-product-compliance
Lightning Source LLC
Chambersburg PA
CBHW071541030726
47598CB00001B/178